Other Titles by Claire Fullerton

A Portal in Time

Claire Fullerton

Dancing to an Irish Reel

Claire Fullerton

Vinspire Publishing
www.vinspirepublishing.com

ISBN: 978-0-9903042-5-8

PUBLISHED BY VINSPIRE PUBLISHING, LLC

To Shirley, who hung the moon

Prologue

There's a road in Spiddal that leads down to the sea. It's lonesome as it meanders between an ancient Catholic church and miles of green, rolling fields separated into geometric prisms by gray stone walls. The gravel on its path is scattered from wind and rain and years of neglect; it is part of the ambience of Spiddal, part of its history. At the end of the road is the Spiddal Pier. There is no sign that would indicate this, but it's common knowledge—like a lot of things on the western coast of Ireland. I didn't know when I first saw the pier that its purpose is twofold: to serve as a port for anglers, and to hold the temperamental Atlantic at bay. Nor did I know, when I first saw the pier, it would become the setting for one of the more memorable episodes of my life.

As many things in Ireland do, this story starts with the music. It may seem a little strange to hear of a single American female living out in the middle of rural Connemara in a village called Inverin, but it just so happened I was there for a reason. I was an employee of the Galway Music Centre, and was there to make a difference in the lives of the local musicians because of my previous experience in the record business in Los Angeles. The fact that I spent nine months in Ireland illegally is not something I aspired to do; it was just something that evolved when I took a sabbatical from my job and decided to visit Ireland on my own in the month of April.

I had simply walked into The Galway Music Centre out of curiosity after reading about its recent opening in the local newspaper, and fell into a casual conversation about popular music with the twenty-five-year-old Irish lad who ran the Centre. His eyes grew wide as I told him about my experience in the record business, and I couldn't have been more surprised when he offered me a job right there on the spot. The truth is, as time went on, I didn't use the return portion of the round-trip ticket I had in my suitcase, thirteen miles up the road in the holiday home I rented in Inverin.

I didn't use it because there was too much happening at the Centre; I was having too good a time, and before I was fully aware of the potential repercussions, I was firmly ensconced in Ireland. In mulling my whole situation over, I decided there was no point in returning to Los Angeles unless I wanted to stay in the LA music business, which I didn't. I kept thinking in five short years I'd be thirty, and if I didn't watch out, I'd wake up one morning to discover I'd put down permanent roots in that big, soulless city. At another time, when I'd realized I'd become disenchanted with Los Angeles, I considered moving back to Memphis, where I'd grown up, but eventually decided that would be a retrograde movement. Since I'd ruled both places out, and since things were going so well for me in Ireland, I figured I'd take the path of least resistance and just go on and stay.

Although the Galway Music Centre was only a fledgling business when I first joined its forces, its vision was resplendent with unbridled faith and enthusiastic ambition generated from the energy of two Irish locals alongside an American academic. They were all brimming with youth and the-sky's-the-limit aspirations; Galway is the kind of place where you can have all that and actually create something from it, for it possesses the alchemical mixture of a vibrant college town in a subtle, rural environment.

In the early days, the four of us spent most our time refurbishing an old iron forge on New Road, and it wasn't long at all before we'd created a musical mecca with an open-door policy dedicated to furthering the careers of the Irish musicians in the area. By day, Declan, Shannon, Darren, and I would hang out in the Centre's courtyard holding cigarettes alongside cups of Barry's Irish Gold tea no matter the capricious Irish weather, while we'd plot the careers of those who gravitated toward us. By night, we'd take to the city streets of Galway in search of either the live music or the "craic," which is what the Irish say when they're talking about having fun. Whichever came first suited us just fine; we quickly became the best of friends who never felt the need to draw the line between work and play.

Chapter One

The Lisheen is a dark, wooden bar on the inside, painted bright orange on the outside. Sandwiched within a row of evenly matched structures in varying primary colors on Galway's High Street, it is one of the many places the four of us frequented when we'd go looking for the craic. Its two rooms are large and spacious with high ceilings and a massive bar against the entry's left wall. Across from the bar, a second room flows to the right where a low stage rises from the wooden floor splattered with tables and chairs that are never enough to accommodate the volume of people who flock to hear the Irish traditional music.

The musicians who grace the stage are of the highest caliber; they are the local players who know the music like the backs of their hands because it's been passed down from previous generations and lives and breathes in their very blood.

Late on a Thursday night, the four of us entered. While they elbowed in at the bar, I followed the lure of the music, weaving my way through the cacophonous crowd until I could finally see the band without obstruction. Beneath a vague spotlight, a fiddler, an accordion player, and a thrashing rhythmic guitarist were spaced on the stage, seemingly in their own world, connected by an emanating force, oblivious to the audience. I stood taking it all in, listening as the tunes created their own personality, setting the mood in rhythms that sounded like laughter. I watched transfixed from my place in the crowd because something about one of them magnetized me, as if I'd known him from somewhere before, yet couldn't place him.

I read somewhere that the entire story waiting to happen is contained within the first moment of contact, just as a seed is to the plant it will eventually become. Perhaps this best explains the uncanny feeling that shot straight through me the first time I laid eyes on Liam Hennessey. He sat holding an accordion upon his knee, lovingly fingering its round, black buttons. With subtle gestures, the nod of his head, the tap of his foot, a swift, indiscernible glance, he set the pace for the other musicians on stage as if by telepathy. For some inexplicable reason, I felt familiar with his dark good looks, black Irish, as the locals say, and the feeling absolutely haunted me.

I stood, trying to recall when I had ever been so intrigued with the look of a stranger. He had an almost feminine beauty: tall and graceful with straight, jet-black hair and dark eyes beneath thick brows like etchings on porcelain. His face was pensive and defined, with a transported gaze as if he were peering beyond the room and into another world. I couldn't shake the feeling I'd either seen him somewhere before, or perhaps presciently, would see him somewhere in the near future. For a few days afterward, the image of the accordion player sprang to me unbidden, for he was that memorable. Then, as you do, I put him in the back of my mind and carried on with the rhythm of my life in Ireland.

It seemed I lived a dual existence in Ireland: there were my days spent in the town of Galway filled with people coming and going through the music centre and then there were my nights and weekends spent mostly alone in the remoteness of Inverin. The dichotomy was pronounced in my first few months in Ireland since I was new to the region and just starting to learn my way around. My rented holiday home had a glassed-in, tile-floored porch where a lone wooden table and four matching chairs held pride of place.

A rectangular window endowed the common wall of the porch and the living room, so no matter which room I was in, it always seemed I was sitting outside with nothing to shield me from the vagaries of Irish weather except for the heavy sliding glass door. The door rocked with the wind and amplified the rain, but on fair days, the porch became a solar-heated haven. I would sit on the porch at the end of the day, admiring the view of the fields that led down to the sea and writing in the spiral notebook I kept as a journal.

Keeping a journal was a habitual pastime in Inverin, along with walking aimlessly through the expansive bog that lay behind my home and ambling through the vast, stone-partitioned fields all the way down to the sea in front of me. On clear days, I would stand at the water's edge and look out toward the Aran Islands and the Cliffs of Moher, and I incrementally developed a kinship with the area, borne from leisurely walking the land in a region that has more soul than any place I ever imagined.

Mick Folan lived deep in the bog behind me, which begins with a slight incline and then levels out as far as the eye can see upon incessant turf and bracken interrupted by a meandering stream that snakes its way through sporadic, mismatched houses. I'd passed him twice before while walking through the bog and had given an uncommitted salutary nod, as you would if you wanted to acknowledge someone's presence, yet nothing more. It's permissible to give a halfhearted nod if you live in a big city, but it's inexcusable in Inverin—that was what I didn't know then.

The thing about living in Inverin is a quick nod is perceived as dismissive and rude. You're not supposed to keep to yourself, and nobody cares if you're not in the mood to socialize. By virtue of the fact that you live in Inverin, you're automatically a part of a collective identity that operates under the assumption that all of its inhabitants are members of the same tribe. It took me a while to realize this, as nobody actually articulates the implication, but I learned it's one of the nuances of rural Irish life, and I discovered quickly there were more rocks underneath that boulder.

The third time I encountered Mick in the bog, he put both hands on his hips and abruptly blocked my path in nonnegotiable body language. I could tell by his stance he'd had entirely enough of not knowing my story, that it had gone on for way too long in his opinion, and it was time to obtain the facts. We began our friendship by commenting on the weather. Mick tilted his head skyward and observed, "Ah, she's blowin' all right." We next got down to the exchange of names, and I learned he already knew where I lived because there is no place to hide in Inverin; word has a way of traveling with lightning speed, and a single American female living in a place like Inverin is big news.

To my surprise, it only took Mick about five minutes to invite me to "call out" for a cup of tea the following day. In Ireland, people are always "calling out," which shouldn't be confused with either a planned arrangement or just showing up, because calling out lays somewhere between, in the realm of "I'll get there when I get there." He seemed endearingly anxious for me to meet his girlfriend, Gabrielle, so I tried to seal the deal by saying I'd come around two in the afternoon. "Don't put a time on it," Mick replied, furrowing his brow. "Come when it suits you."

I had two thoughts as I continued my walk through the bog that day, and the first concerned the weather. I puzzled it through until I understood why the weather is personified as "she" in Ireland. It's because "she" is so pervasive, and for a population that lives at the dictates of weather, when people in Ireland say "she," everyone knows what is meant. The second thought on my mind was the astounding lackadaisical attitude Mick had regarding when I would appear for tea. His attitude illustrated the open-armed way the Irish have of receiving everyone. There is always an open door, and they are always sitting at the ready, happy to invite you in to a comfortable seat by the fire.

We sat in Mick's kitchen the following day because it was the warmest room in the house. Its floor was made of reddish-brown brick, and a chipped, green-painted table sat beneath the eastern window. Through the window, unending bog stretched out forever, save for the cat drolly staring in from the windowsill. Quietly from a rocking chair, Gabrielle cradled their son Solas, which is the Irish word for sun, while Mick and I traded turns either standing before the fire, or sitting on the hand-woven rug before the hearth. A teakettle warmed inside the fireplace as we traded personal histories, mine as a newcomer to the area, Mick's, as a transplant from Clonmel in County Tipperary, and Gabrielle's involving a move to Ireland, two years before from France.

Mick put a log on the fire, poured us all a cup of tea, and settled down comfortably in his tattered, upholstered chair. Speaking in a hushed, reverential tone, he held me captive with his eyes.

"It's wicked powerful out here in Inverin, so it is," he said, narrowing his eyes to half-mast and looking straight through me. "The power, ye see, comes from the monolithic dolmen way in the bog behind us. Because of it, Inverin is literally an energy center on our planet. We're all affected by the energy out here, and we're all a part of that energy as well. In fact, it's that energy that connects us, one to the other." I followed along wordlessly.

"See, Inverin is on a ley line," he continued. "You can think of the dolmen as an acupuncturist's needle marking a spot on the earth where energy pulses. Ley lines serve as healing centers no matter what needs to be healed: body, mind, or spirit. All ye have to do is come into her field, and healed you'd be from her very presence." Mick had such total conviction, that I blindly believed every word he said.

"Have you found the dolmen yet?" Mick studied me. I admitted I had not. "Well, I'd show you meself, but I'd rather it be your own journey. This is your time for discovery, and I wouldn't be the one to get in the way. Just remember, we're as steeped in magic and mysticism today as our ancestors ever were. When the time is right, you'll find the dolmen, sure as you're sitting here with your cup of tea." He nodded toward my cup.

I looked down at my teacup, registering Mick's explanation, then allowed my gaze to survey the room as something dawned on me: there seems to be a rampant theme to a rural Irish kitchen. Most of the ones I've been in are in complete shambles. It appears to be on purpose. If you look around an Irish kitchen, what you notice most is nothing matches, nor is anything completely put away. Rather, things are simply shoved aside in order to make room for the next order of business, whatever that may be; once that business is completed, further responsibility in the room is vacated altogether.

Also, everything looks old and worn: the spices, the utensils, the cookware, the countertop, even the walls of an Irish kitchen. It's as though everything has just always been there. It is nothing short of a haphazard arrangement, which is exactly what makes an Irish kitchen so inviting. I looked back at Mick, gathering a sense of his constitution. Usually a person has to be a lot older to have the kind of character he possessed at the surprising age of twenty-six. His was the kind of personality typically grown organically and cultivated over a lifetime, as if earned from years of grueling experience, so I found his soulful, grounded demeanor unusual in someone so young.

What struck me the most about Mick was that his awareness level was practically tangible; if I stood close enough to him, I could feel the wheels of his mind turning. He sent out an energetic pulse from a youthful face with clear blue eyes and a fair complexion that would no doubt freckle if he stayed in the sun too long. He was tall and delicately thin, with a thick black frame of long, wavy hair that was always in movement. He was forthright, focused, and intensely passionate; when coalesced, these characteristics made for astonishing storytelling abilities.

The conversation turned when Mick started talking about an old graveyard that lay halfway down a gravel lane leading to the sea. The lane was immediately across the street from where I lived, and I'd walked down it many times because something about it was so desolately inviting. The hill where the graveyard lay descended to a ledge above the sea, and all the tombstones faced the dramatic water as it crashed against the boulders below.

"Why do you think that is, Mick? Why line up graves in a row and point them to the sea?" I wanted to know.

"So all the bodies of the dead can pay homage to the

sea, which is Ireland's lifeblood," he said. "There's your answer plain and simple. All the ancient names in this area of Connemara lay in those graves, but they've no intention of ever resting." Mick folded his hands together and leaned forward in his chair. "That entire lane there is haunted, don't cha know, and a brave soul it would be who would walk that path alone at night."

"Have you ever done it?" Gabrielle asked Mick with a note of concern.

"I have." Mick quickly met her gaze, "But believe me, no woman would ever want to."

They say there are four seasons in one day in Ireland for a good reason. Like spontaneous combustion, the sky opened up without warning and pelted down thunderous sheets of rain that banged on the roof and turned everything a deeper shade of eggplant with each hovering cloud. Running for dear life from the front door to Mick's tan-colored van, I jumped in quickly, then Mick jostled his way through the bog and deposited me at my door.

"I'd call you, but I've cut meself off from the phone." Mick leaned halfway out the window, not seeming to care about the stinging rain. "I can't trust meself anymore; too many late-night calls on the drink running up me phone bill, so I rigged it where people can call in, but I can't call out." I thought that sounded a little weird, but I wasn't going to stand around in the rain taking issue. I told Mick I'd be in touch and ducked into the shelter of my porch.

Later that night, after the rain let up, I put on a warm coat and stepped outside my door. I stood in the darkened stillness until I'd made up my mind once and for all. There are no streetlights that far out in Inverin, but I had the faint light of a waxing moon. Cautiously, I crossed the coast road. I heard the gravel scratching beneath my steps and put one foot in front of the other in a cadence that sounded like a military march. A slight wind blew like a whisper, then rushed suddenly, just enough to startle me before it ebbed again.

I thought I felt a chill on the back of my neck and wondered if it was the night air or just my fear. Down the lane I continued, until the graveyard loomed up on the hill to my left. Granite tombstones of varying heights crowned with Celtic crosses glowed in the moonlight. It was a graveyard forever marking time, halfway down a lane all but forgotten. I walked steadily, not daring to stop, not wanting to hesitate, only wanting to walk the lane at night because Mick had said no woman would want to.

Chapter Two

The mornings in Inverin are hushed. Everything is in a state of becoming, waiting for the steel-gray sky to turn to light. It takes hours no matter the time of year, for the day comes on in stages. The light only suggests itself at first, coming and going behind moving clouds until it is finally full-on. Most mornings, I readied myself to go into Galway the same way: I'd put a pound in the wall meter for electricity, heat water in the electric kettle for tea, fold layers of striped, heavy woolen blankets across my bed, and fill my brown leather backpack with the day's necessities. Once pulled together, I'd walk to the end of my driveway and wait at the unmarked side of the road, across the street from the Centra grocery store. That's what you do in rural Ireland: you just stand out on the coast road when you want a lift into town and stare expectantly at the bus driver when you see the bus coming.

On Sundays, I knew the bus heading into Galway would happen around three in the afternoon. The problem was the only Sunday bus leaving Galway and heading out past Inverin also happened around three, but that's rural Ireland for you. I pulled out my Ray-Bans and looked up the road in anticipation of Bus Eireann's encroachment from the closest little village of Carraroe to the north. Declan would be predictably irritated when he saw me. I was sure of what he'd say in his clipped, Northern Irish accent.

"Would ye take off those damn sunglasses so I can talk to youse!" We'd been through it a couple of times before. I decided to worry about Declan and getting home later as I climbed into the bus.

The bus was one of those old kinds that looked like it had once enjoyed life as an elementary-school bus, but had been put out to pasture. With sliding glass windows and aluminum handrails on the seats before, it took off noisily, the gravel beneath its tires scattering before there was a chance to sit down. The bus driver had taken to greeting me in stilted English. He had picked me up many times before and spoken to me in Irish, the first language of the region, but upon realizing I am American, he settled upon greeting me with a nod and the only word he seemed to know in English, which came out sounding something like a guttural, "Hiya."

I actually liked riding the bus into Galway. It was an encapsulated, traveling theatrical show typically staged with the same cast of characters. It seemed everybody knew the bus driver personally, because everyone would stop and chat forever once they got on. Looking out the window, I'd see people strolling along the sides of the road, smiling and waving as the bus passed them by. I wondered if everybody in town knew the bus driver socially, perhaps having him to their homes for tea, or if they just waved perfunctorily, much in the way they'd perform the holy sign of the cross every time we passed a church. Because I was new to the area, these were the kinds of thoughts that occupied my mind. I stood up at the stop near the Spanish Arch in Galway, signaling my intention of dismounting.

There is a feel about Galway you can wear around your shoulders like a cloak. It hangs in the air with its dampness; it walks the cobblestone streets and stands in the doorways of its gray stone buildings. It blows in with the mist from the Atlantic and lingers incessantly at every corner. I have never been able to walk the streets of

Galway without feeling some unnamed presence accompanying me. It's a disconcerting feeling—a little like knowing you're being watched. I made my way up Quay Street, turned left, and crossed O'Brien's bridge on the way to Shannon's rented flat.

Shannon lived on Nun's Island Road in Mrs. Donoghue's boarding house, which rose up from the sidewalk in cold gray stone positioned among a row of similar structures. The wooden door was painted green, and the two windows overhead were adorned with white lace. I knocked on the door using its large brass knocker. After a time it swung wide, and there stood Mrs. Donoghue. She was a tall, thin, slightly stooped crone in her seventies with weathered white skin and watery blue eyes. Mrs. Donoghue was the owner and self-appointed gatekeeper of Number One, Nuns Island Road. In order to get to Shannon, one had to go through Mrs. Donoghue, and every time I tried, I had to reintroduce myself, for Mrs. Donoghue was the forgetful sort.

"Hello, Mrs. Donoghue," I said. "I'm Hailey Crossan, I'm here to see Shannon."

"Shannon, is it? Let me see." She closed the door in front of me with a sharp catch. After ten minutes of waiting, I walked out into the street and called up to the lace-covered curtains. Shannon's head quickly appeared though the window.

"Oh, there you are," Shannon said, "come on up."

"Will you remind Mrs. Donoghue of who I am?" I said looking up, palms out in an exasperated shrug. "She's seen me three times before; this is ridiculous."

"I know," Shannon said. "It's okay, just walk right in."

I found Shannon, Darren, and Declan in the kitchen that lay to the right at the top of the stairs. There was barely room for the three of them in the cramped makeshift kitchen, cluttered to the rafters with pots, pans, and mismatched chairs around a square table, a microwave, a hotplate, electric kettle, and way too many other implements to identify, so as soon as I arrived, we took to the roof, climbing out through the window that sat halfway up the stairs. For the next two hours, we watched Galway's yearly Macnas Parade wind through the streets below, decked out in thematic theatrical costumes to rival New Orleans' Mardi Gras beneath a light, steady rain. Declan, being the man on the case at all times, disappeared through the window and returned with an umbrella big enough to shelter him, Shannon, and me while Darren sat nearby, his back against the gray stone chimney, his head protected from the rain by a nameless baseball cap.

Although intrigued by the spectacle below, my gaze kept shifting to the three beside me: first Shannon Forester, an American from Dallas and a student at the University of California, Los Angeles. She was two years in Galway for the purpose of writing her thesis on ethnomusicology, and had chosen the Galway Music Centre as her field case study, which made her the administrative arm of the outfit because she was so organized. She was beautiful and mysterious, with an economic way of speaking that always made me wonder what was left unsaid.

With a look like a young Faye Dunaway, Shannon possessed an innate maturity that went well beyond her twenty-seven years, and although she appeared aloof, she was actually accessible and warmhearted. Then there was Darren Thornton: tall, golden blond, and genteel, wearing a baseball cap in the spattering rain that was incongruous to everything about his courtly, refined demeanor. Six foot one and extremely well-spoken with an accent that rolled like an Oxford-educated scholar, Darren came to Galway with his older brother for the singular experience of leaving London.

Being born of Irish parents from Sligo, Ireland who had relocated to London, Galway seemed like a feasible town for this twenty-four-year-old to investigate. That was the extent of Darren's plan up until the moment he bumped into Shannon, with whom he was clearly in love. He had a curious mixture of grace and bravado; he was well mannered, yet opinionated; elegant, yet a true man's man. He had the air of a gentleman of leisure, yet the first time I saw Darren, he had his shirt peeled off and a hammer in his hand as he nailed the railing together of the staircase leading up to the loft in the Galway Music Centre. Darren leaned casually against the chimney, smoking a Silk Cut cigarette.

"Would you like a fag?" Darren said to nobody in particular.

It is customary in Ireland to offer everyone in the group a cigarette from the pack you extend. It is like offering a gift, cigarettes being the expense they are, and what the one offering at the moment is actually doing is picking up the tab for his friends. It's a little like buying a round of drinks, but on a smaller scale. I accepted a Silk Cut from the pack Darren held out.

"Are you on the heavies?" Darren asked, ending the sentence with the emphasis on the word "heavies." I had not realized the color on the pack was purple.

"Here, I have a blue." Shannon traded me a heavy for a light.

"The Music Centre should put on a show like this," Declan said, peering down at the sight of the parade as it made its promenade in loud, ringing noises through the center of town. I looked over at Declan, taking note of the fact that he always thought on a large scale. He was technically the head of the Galway Music Centre since the venture had been his idea, so he liked to call all the shots. His last name was Fenton, and he had moved from Derry to Galway three months before to make something of himself. Of course, it occurred to me after knowing him for a short period of time that Declan had moved into Galway to take over completely; he had that kind of a personality.

He was a quick-talking, high-strung, plan-making twenty-five-year-old with a Northern Irish accent that was so quick and guttural, it verged on being unintelligible. Declan could not walk down the streets of Galway without something happening, and when he wasn't out in the streets, activity had a way of coming to him. He was a vortex of frenetic, creative energy that was always in the works, and he frequently plotted his next move before his current plan had been hatched. Slightly yet compactly built, Declan was the product of an Irish father and a Chinese mother, which made a fascinating combination.

He looked Chinese, yet was tall with coarse, dark hair which he wore in a high ponytail that bobbed joyously behind him, swinging like a pendulum from right to left then left to right. He shaved the front and sides of his head in an effort at showing his ponytail off, and although it made him look like a punk, according to Declan, it was his symbol of individuality. There was always an enigmatic, mischievous look on Declan's face. Even in repose, he looked like he was up to something. His small, slightly upturned, oval, black eyes would either twinkle with amusement, or bore a hole right through you, depending on his mood at the moment. He was a bit of a loose cannon, but I always thought when Declan found his niche in life, when he actually became focused, it was going to be big.

"Right," Darren continued sarcastically, cocking his head toward Declan, "we'll just take the extra thousand quid we have lying around and put on a parade."

"I'm not talking about a parade, you cowboy, I'm talking about a show," Declan shot back, defensively.

"A show isn't a bad idea as long as it would showcase the musicians we know," I pointed out, coming to Declan's side. "It would give them exposure, and help us get the word around about what's happening at the Centre."

"We would have a lot to organize," Shannon said in that succinct way of hers. "First of all, we'd need to find a place to hold it." She looked at Darren, who nodded his agreement.

"And we'll have to hire a PA for sound," Darren said.

"We'd have to think of charging a fee that would include giving a bit to the venue," Shannon, ever the pragmatist, continued.

"We can call out to Paul at the Kings Head tomorrow and chat to him about doing it there," Declan said. "It's not easy getting a time slot there—may take months, but once we do, Hailey can decide which musicians to put on stage."

"Easy," I responded. "I've already got a few in mind."

"All right mates, fair enough, we'll all go tomorrow and get things rolling," Darren concluded.

"Hailey, aren't you going to meet Leigh McDonough tomorrow morning?" Declan interrogated in his best authoritarian voice.

"I was planning on it," I said.

"Call out to the Centre afterward, and we'll go from

there," he instructed.

I arrived in Galway at ten the following morning and navigated the winding cobblestone sidewalk to a little diner called the Left Bank Café. Pushing through the glass door, its string of aluminum red bells jingling to announce my entrance, I spotted Leigh McDonough at a Formica table with a plate of brown bread, which is customarily served throughout Ireland, and a pot of tea before her. She stood up when she saw me, giving me a clear view of her unbuttoned flannel shirt, which flapped lazily over a ribbed tank top and rumpled, olive cargo pants that were rolled at the ankle to expose flip-flops as if she'd just crawled off a beach.

"I'm not late, am I?" I said, pulling out a chair.

"Ah, God, no," Leigh said, "I got here early. We Aussie's are always a step ahead of the game. How ya going there?" she said in a finely clipped accent.

"I'm all right," I returned.

Leigh arched back in her chair and shook her head, then threw her sun-bleached, gnarled dreadlocks back to catch them in a faded red bandana, which she tied messily on top of her head.

"All right, let's get down to business," she said, leaning forward, elbows on the table. "I've got one day to lay down the foundation of three—maybe four good songs. I'm leaving for Cork tomorrow so there'll be no mucking about. I want you just listening, getting an overview because some of the arrangements are in question. Can you do that?"

"Of course," I said. "I can be objective. I'll just act like an audience member."

"I want you to be a critic." Leigh looked me in the eyes. "Give it to me straight. You'll be a sounding board.

I'm too close to my songs to be objective. I know you've got a good musical feel. You've got good sensibilities. I want this to all come out like power pop with a little something more."

"Okay, I'll give it to you straight," I said, "but I'm already a fan along with everybody else in Ireland. It's no surprise why you sell out everywhere you play. You know who you remind me of? Fiona Apple, the quality of your voice is similar, that sultry edge. Also, there's that tendency to write unambiguous lyrics, I love that."

"That's another Australian quality, we all stay on point. It's what's called convict mentality, none of us mess around."

"I'll give you that, it's why Declan doesn't know what to make of you."

"Ah, there," she said. "Declan. Well, he's not sure what to make of women, is he? That's all right. He fancies himself a businessman. All he heard is I'm paying a fair quid to steal you away for the day."

"Astute point about Declan, but I think you're the kind of woman men see as a challenge anyway because you meet them on equal footing."

"And I'm older than Declan. I'm thirty-five. No point in trying to patsy around with me," she said, laughing. Leigh looked at her wristwatch. "Let me pay at the counter. You can meet me at the van. My keyboard and guitar are in it so it's locked; here's the key. It's the red one on the corner. We should get going. Oranmore is about forty minutes away."

There is a secret language musicians speak that does away with the need for articulation because it is intuitive and telepathic at its core. Tom Reynolds and the handful of other musicians who sat cloistered in the happy hunting ground of the studio bringing Leigh's record to life employed it with subtlety, and I was fascinated. A chord progression on a keyboard was accompanied by a sideways glance with a raised eyebrow from Leigh, and it was completely understood a question had been posited, which elicited either a Cheshire smile or a furrowed brow from Tom in lieu of words.

I felt as if I were in an insular bubble, privy to the secret internal mechanisms of a musician's rarified gift, and was spellbound and awed by an experience few non-musicians are ever privy to. I sat in the background thinking something ineffable resides within the soul of a musician that specifically classifies them, yet paradoxically sets them apart from the rest of humanity. I've always had the impression musicians are just fine with it, even though it's the rare one who'd ever feel the need to explain themselves to a layman. I think if musicians were inclined to explain, they'd tell you nothing on earth matters to them more than music, and they'd keep it as simple as that. This was the valuable insight I walked away with that day, while Leigh walked away with four recorded songs that stand the test of time.

The road from Oranmore to Inverin is long and uneventful, but Leigh and I were so exhilarated from the ten hours we'd spent laying the foundation for her record that we barely noticed the length of time. We gave Tom Reynolds a lift into Galway, then headed up the coast in the ten o'clock hour of a Saturday night, pulling off the road as we entered Spiddal. At night, Spiddal can seem like a ghost town, but that's only because most of its activity lies behind closed doors. There are precious few buildings lining the main street, but what little is there stands closely together.

What is worth mentioning in Spiddal is the old church, the Spiddal Pier, the hackney office, the post office tucked away in the back of the grocery store, and two quaint hotels. Across the street from one of the hotels is a restaurant called the Cruiscan Lan, which means "little jug of whisky" in Irish. Its front door faces the coast road as it passes through Spiddal, and at its back is a glassed-in area that faces the sea. Were the Cruiscan, as it is called locally, in any other place than Spiddal, there might have been lights out back and perhaps a deck for viewing the sea, but that is not the way it is with the Cruiscan.

Contrarily, one merely has the sense that the sea lies out back, and it would be completely incidental were it not for the intrusion of its sonic ambiance. Inside the Cruiscan, a dark, narrow entrance hall with a small room off its left promenades into a large room with a prominent bar that stands sentry at the junction where another room opens up for performance space. The walls of the room are lined with leather-covered benches, and there are no windows to speak of. Although it started out as a restaurant, the Cruiscan quickly became a musical venue where anything from Irish traditional music to original songwriters could be heard along with a regularly scheduled night of set-dancing. As opposed to Hughes, the other pub in Spiddal, the Cruiscan became a place where children are welcomed as well. Whether or not that was the initial plan, the locals christened it as such, and therefore it became so.

Leigh and I were not long inside the Cruiscan before the two salt-of-the-earth men at the bar started "chatting me up," as they say in Ireland. They'd been unabashedly watching us from the moment we walked through the door. I've never known what it is that makes some men think unescorted women are fair game, but I can't say I didn't see it coming. I could feel it on the back of my neck before I spotted them with my peripheral vision. They were "on the piss," as it's nationally called when someone intentionally and unapologetically sets out to get rip-roaring drunk. One of the men reached out and grabbed my arm as Leigh and I passed by. It's funny how things hit you at different times in different places. In most cases, an unwarranted gesture like that would be scary or offensive, but because it was rural Ireland, I only saw the humor. The two men may have been on the piss, but they were harmless; I knew it intuitively.

"What brings a lovely thing like you here this night?" one of them asked—the one who was holding my arm.

"We're just passing through," I said, turning to face him.

"Are you long here?" he asked, emphasizing the word *long.*

Am I long where? I thought. *Am I long at the Cruiscan? Am I long in Spiddal? Am I long in Ireland? This is no doubt a translation issue,* I thought. *Anyway, does he mean have I been here long, or do I intend to stay here long?* My mind was racing. It was not the first time I'd been asked that question in Ireland, it seemed to be part and parcel to an Irish introduction, something commonly asked after the extension of "Nice to meet you." Rather than risking embarrassment by asking what the question meant, I was in the habit of bluffing my way through the answer, hoping to appear as if I understood the question.

There are many idioms flying around Connemara that have their origin in the Irish language; I'm pretty sure "Are you long here?" is one of them. The thing is, when asked in any other language but Irish, I can't help but think something is missing.

"I live here," I returned, "I live in Inverin." I had the feeling if you see someone once in Connemara, you're going to see them repeatedly, so I might as well tell the truth.

"What is it that brings you to Inverin?" he asked, finally releasing my arm.

I told him I was working for the Galway Music Centre. "And I'm working on a book of poetry; I'm a poet," I said.

"Ah, aren't we all," he said, then he winked and lifted his pint.

I looked over my shoulder trying to locate Leigh. When I spotted her, she was at the bar talking to a young man named Kieran Murphy, whom I'd initially met in Galway and wasn't at all surprised to see thirteen miles away at the Cruiscan. Kieran Murphy had a way of being everywhere. It didn't matter where I was, it always seemed he beat me there. For someone who didn't own a car, he was remarkably mobile.

Kieran was originally from Dundalk, but had moved to Spiddal two years before to follow in his grandfather's footsteps, which involved the manual art of roof thatching, a trade in which he seemed to be steadily employed. That's what Kieran did during the day; at night he prowled around looking for action. I extricated myself from the two men at the bar, joined Leigh and Kieran, then the three of us found a table in the back beside the window facing the sea. For the next hour and a half, Kieran entertained us with Irish anecdotes, Irish history, Irish legends, and demonstrations of the Irish language, so charmingly proud was he of his heritage. The more Guinness he drank, the funnier he got, but by the fourth pint, Leigh and I started sneaking each other that covert look that signals it's time to wrap things up.

"Right then, it's time to hit the road," Leigh said. I pushed out my chair and stood up.

"Oh, no, not yet," Kieran entreated. "You can't leave yet, it's just half eleven; Hughes will be just starting up. Youse have to come with me."

"Kieran, it's getting late, it's been a long day and—" I began.

"Have you ever been to Hughes on a Sunday night?" he looked at me with pleading eyes.

"Kieran, we have to go." Leigh sounded final.

"Please," Kieran said, "the best trad music in these parts is right across the street. Just come with me for a little while."

"Maybe another time," Leigh deflected, but I looked at her, rolled my eyes, and conceded, "It's going to be easier to walk across the street for a minute than to keep going around in circles with this." We filed out of the Cruiscan and walked across the unlighted coast road.

Hughes, locally pronounced "Hughes-ez," has a long history of sheltering generations beneath its one room roof. Were it not for Kieran, I would never have noticed the pub, nor the insignificant road where it lay. There is no structural asset to Hughes, save for its fireplace and a full bar, yet the locals go there night after night. They go for the drink, and they go for the company. When we got there, the place was packed. Music wafted from the corner, loud voices rang, and there was no place to sit.

What I realize now is how the three of us must have looked: we were two strangers entering local territory with a young man that everybody knew. Leigh and I were a curiosity; I could feel a few eyes watching us from a distance, sizing us up, trying to determine who was with whom. As it turned out, one pair of eyes watching us belonged to someone I had watched before.

Chapter Three

There's an energy that hangs between strangers even in a crowd. Call it interest or attraction or the knowledge of things to come. It is awareness, and I was aware to the exclusion of all activity around me that Liam Hennessey was watching me. He was sitting at the corner of the bar by himself, and because I could feel his gaze upon me like an electrical current, I froze. I did not move an inch because I sensed I didn't have to, that something would come about with little prompting from me. I don't know how I knew this, but I was right, it came about within the hour. It began as a series of introductions to people near Liam and drew itself closer until Liam was introduced to me.

Right before Leigh left, claiming she had to get up early the next day to drive to Cork, Kieran pointed out that the Irish traditional musicians playing in the corner were the father and older brother of the lad sitting at the end of the bar.

"That's Liam Hennessey at the bar there." Kieran gestured to my right. "He's the best box player in Connemara—even in the whole of Ireland, many say. His family is long in Connemara; they're all players, so. That's Sean Liam, his da, and his brother Anthony there on the guitar." Kieran seemed proud to know the facts. He next took my arm and led me straight to Liam, and as he did so, I contemplated his charming use of the word "so" at the end of his sentence. I'd heard it before in Connemara, and realized it was a shortened version of "so it is," which I found to be a good example of how the Irish verify their own speech.

"I've the pleasure of knowing this American here; her name is Hailey," Kieran announced to Liam.

I had an uneasy feeling. It's one thing to suspect you'll cross paths with someone again, and quite another to be fully prepared when it actually happens. For some unknown reason, I kept thinking it was strange to see Liam this far out in the country from Galway, but then again, what did I know? I didn't know anything about him.

Liam looked at me with large dark eyes and smiled brightly. He was different than I had imagined; he was friendlier, more candid. I assumed because he looked so dark and mysterious, there would be a personality to match. I assumed he would be reserved, aloof, perhaps arrogant in an artistic sort of way. I was paying close attention, and there was none of that about Liam. In seconds, I realized he was a nice guy. I moved a step to my right as an older man approached the bar.

"Would ye give us a hand there," the man said to Liam, and for the next few minutes, Liam handed pints over his head to a group of men too far from the bar's edge to grab the glasses themselves. Just then, Kieran said something that set off a chain of events and put the rest of the night in motion.

"Liam, will you watch Hailey for me? I'm off to join the session." With that, Kieran produced a harmonica from his shirt pocket and walked off to join the musicians in the corner.

I stood at the bar and waited for the next thing to happen. The world seemed to operate in slow motion. All the noise in the room subsided, and the only thing I knew was I was looking directly at Liam Hennessey. I searched his face for imperfections. I had never before seen such beauty in the face of a man. I hoped my thoughts didn't show on my face. He was so good-looking, I wondered why other people in the room weren't staring at him; then I realized most of Hughes' patrons knew him and were probably used to the way he looked. I was reticent, unsure of how to speak to Liam, unfamiliar with how provincial he may or may not have been. Words tend to get in the way in moments like this, but they lay in wait just the same.

"You're an American, yah?" he asked in that way the Irish have of answering their own question. "I've been to America," he said.

"Where in America?" I encouraged.

"Boston, New York, Chicago. My cousins live in Chicago. I even went all the way to Niagara Falls."

"Believe it or not, I've never been to Niagara Falls. What's it like?"

"Not much, mind you, it's a nice enough place, but ten minutes after I saw the falls, I was asking where I could get a nice cup of tea."

"I imagine it would take a lot to be impressed after living here," I said.

"I'd never want to live anywhere else. Everything you could ever want is here in Connemara."

And it is, I thought. *Connemara has a sense of peace I've never felt before.*

"Are you long in Ireland?" he asked.

"I live here," I said. "I live in Inverin."

"Ah, so you're just up the road. Me, too."

At twenty-seven years old, Liam lived with his parents in the house in which he grew up. He was a world-class Irish traditional musician that traveled often to places like Germany, Austria, and New Zealand. He was in demand as a player in touring bands because he was a master at playing the button accordion. As such, he was more than a musician, he was the bearer of a torch that represented the history of an old culture. He brought the language of Irish music to regions that otherwise would have never been enlightened.

Being an Irish traditional musician is a feat painstakingly achieved. Most of the tunes in a traditional player's repertoire have been memorized through listening and repeated execution, as opposed to memorization by reading musical scores. Traditional music has been passed down through generational lines, and with Liam's family, there had been no interruption. His father was a player, and the world in which Liam grew up was one of constant exposure to traditional music as if it were a language. I came to realize much later that Liam's first language was music, his second language was Irish, and his third was English.

"So, you must be another American looking for their roots, then," Liam stated.

If that was a question, then it's a fair one, I thought.

"Actually, I'm working at the Galway Music Center," I said, and then I followed with my poetry aspirations, hoping to impress upon him I was not just passing through.

"Who is your favorite poet?" Liam changed the subject.

"I wouldn't feel good standing here much longer if I didn't say William Butler Yeats. Other than that, I like Lord Byron a lot, and W.H. Auden."

"I haven't read much of Auden, but Byron, now there's someone I know about," Liam said, the glow of enthusiasm springing to his eyes. He then went on to weave the tale of Lord Byron's affair with a woman named Claire Clairmont. I was familiar with the story, but feigned fascination anyhow because I wanted him to keep talking. It didn't escape me how dissimilarly he spoke from other people in Connemara. His accent came close to sounding like the King's English, but because he was Irish, it came out sounding like deliberately enunciated diction riding the crest of an Irish lilt. He hit hard on the consonants, especially when ending a sentence, and there was a formality to his speech that suggested higher education and refinement. It made me all the more curious about him, for he was becoming more incongruous to the region by the minute.

Although the people I'd encountered in Connemara by this time had a charming way of talking, I didn't equate their dialect with the kind of sophistication I heard in Liam's speech. The people in Connemara had a dialect that was flavorfully rich in character. They infused their colloquialisms in a manner that turned a normal phrase into an enviable art form, and it seemed to me their aspirations leaned heavily toward the comedic, which made it absolutely delightful. Because Liam spoke differently, I suspected he was somehow a cut apart from those around him in more ways than his speech.

"Claire Clairmont was at the house party with Lord Byron the night Mary Shelley began the story that later became Frankenstein. It was meant to be an amusement for the guests," Liam said.

"Really!" I said, not wanting to dampen his enthusiasm.

"Oh, yes. I don't believe they had a long affair, but a child was conceived. Byron agreed to care for the child, but decided to have nothing further to do with Claire."

It's funny the thoughts that run through your head while you're talking to someone for the first time. My mind was all over the place trying to size him up, but mostly, I was listening to the way he spoke and trying not to let on that I couldn't get over how good-looking he was. I noticed the musicians in the corner, including Liam's' father, brother, and Kieran, were watching us as if an event were taking place at the bar. A few men sauntered up to Liam trying to appear casual, but I could tell they wanted to investigate as well. It made me feel uneasy, as if I were on display.

Eventually, Kieran ambled over and started engaging Liam. I instantly noticed how drunk he was; he was talking unnecessarily loud and kept leaning in way too close, trying to establish a steady posture. I wished Kieran would just disappear, but I wasn't that lucky. I stood back from the pair when an older man wearing a fisherman's sweater cornered me and started asking me questions about myself. After half an hour of this, I decided it was time to leave.

There is a hackney service a couple of yards away from Hughes, and it was open all night. I decided to be self-sufficient and simply take my leave. I figured it was the only way to lose Kieran because I know when a guy is acting like they're with you, and I wanted to make it plain to Kieran, and more pointedly Liam, that was not the case. After telling Liam it was nice talking to him, I nodded curtly at Kieran because I've never had much of a tolerance for drunks. I walked out of Hughes and headed toward the hackney office. Out in the street, I realized I was being followed, and then I heard my name.

"Hailey, can I walk with you?" Kieran called into the dark. Turning, I let him catch up with me.

"Sure," I said "but I'm just going to the hackney office."

"Why don't you take a walk with me instead?" he asked.

"It's a little late, Kieran, I better get home." I started

walking again.

"Oh come on, it's a lovely night. Walk with me."

"Thanks for the offer, but I really have to go."

Kieran kept following me closely. "Can I come with you?"

"Come with me where?"

"To your place."

"That's not a good idea, Kieran."

"Why not?" he whined.

"For starters, I don't know you that well, Kieran." It wouldn't have mattered what I said at that point; it was turning into one of those circular conversations you can only have with a drunk.

"Well, if I came home with you, that would be a good way to get to know me," Kieran said.

I couldn't believe it. We were standing out on the coast road by the hackney service, right across the street from the church, and there wasn't another soul around. I was thinking this is crazy, I'm just going into the hackney office and that's going to be it when Liam materialized out of thin air. I didn't know what he was doing out on the street, but he came right to me and broke it all up. The three of us stood in the pitch-black night.

"Are you all right?" Liam asked protectively. It seemed he knew I was being pestered.

"I'm fine, but Kieran could use a little help," I said.

Ignoring Kieran, Liam asked pointedly, "What do you want to do?"

"Anything but this," I said. It was better than saying, "I'm going home," taking into account Liam had gone to all the trouble of playing knight in shining armor.

"Come with me," Liam directed.

It was closing time when I followed Liam back to Hughes. The crowd had thinned out considerably, and most of the stragglers were poised to leave. Once we were inside, a ruggedly handsome man who looked to be in his early thirties approached. He smiled quickly at Liam, and stared down at me as if waiting for an introduction.

"This is Patrick," Liam complied. "Patrick, this is Hailey."

"You wear black sunglasses and take the six-o'clock bus out from Galway every afternoon," Patrick said, smiling down at me. I was surprised at that, but then again, the entire night had already been a series of surprises.

Patrick Theid hailed from New Zealand. I liked him right away, before I even learned he was Liam's best friend. He had an imposing presence and a confident air that suggested he was totally in control. On his left cheekbone, a scar was faintly etched, but it somehow complimented his broad, handsome face. He wore his long ash-blond hair swept back from his high forehead in such a way it framed his angular face. His eyes were the color of the sea before a storm, hazy green, mixed with blue gray; they stood out from a complexion that was weathered but not aged. His massive shoulders gave the impression that were he to walk across the room, he would do so with athletic swagger.

"How ya going?" Patrick asked in an accent that sounded a little to the left of Australian.

"It's been an interesting night," I answered. "I'm sorry you couldn't be a part of it."

I looked over my shoulder and noticed Kieran sitting at a bench alongside the front wall. When I looked at him, his face turned red and he cravenly averted his gaze.

"It looks to be closing time," Patrick pointed out.

I started thinking I should try for the hackney service again. "I better get going," I said to them both.

"I'll go with you," Liam volunteered.

Out on the street, Liam turned to me. "I have a car, but I'm afraid to drive it this late—the guards, you know."

I didn't know. "The what?"

"The guards. They'll be out on the road stopping cars."

I got the gist of his meaning.

"We could get a couple of cans anyway, and I'll drive you home," he offered.

"A couple of what?"

"Cans, you know, beer," he clarified.

"Liam, is there a language barrier here? I feel like I need a translator."

"I'm willing to overlook it if you are," he said.

"I think we're going to have to," I said, suppressing a smile.

Liam walked around the corner to the store while I stood out on the dark street looking over my shoulder in case Kieran resurrected. When Liam returned, he was carrying a brown paper bag. "My car is just out back," he gestured.

We rounded the corner to his two-door car, which had a make and model I'd never seen in America.

Liam broke the silence, once we got in the car. "I feel a little awkward."

"Me too," I said, "but it'll be all right."

"Have you ever seen the Spiddal Pier?" he asked suddenly.

"I don't think so," I said. "Maybe I have, but just didn't know it. It's not like there are any signs around here."

Liam drove straight across the coast road until the tires hit the gravel road beside the old church in Spiddal. It was too dark to see more than four yards ahead, so we inched forth to the sound of scattering gravel until the road ended and the Spiddal Pier loomed out of the sea at the left.

You have to climb the Spiddal Pier. It is so huge and its stone is such a dark color of gray that it's not advisable to risk it at night. The wash from the sea as it crashes and sprays over the wall makes it slippery as well. The beginning of it, if you can actually pinpoint the beginning, is only a narrow walkway with a wall jutting up on its right side. There are stairs carved into the structure that once climbed, leave you at an elevation perhaps four feet higher than the walkway, then it gets bigger, growing as you walk in the direction of the sea, opening up until there is a larger area with a ledge that completes the entire structure at a ninety-degree angle.

We sat on the ledge in the freezing night air. There is nothing at the end of the pier to block the wind that blows in from the Atlantic, so it's man against the elements as you sit there on the edge of the wall. It didn't matter to me at the time, and by all appearances, it didn't matter to Liam either. I thought it was a strange spot to begin to get to know each other, but that's where we were: well past midnight on the edge of the Spiddal Pier.

"What do you do in Inverin, or is that a rude question?" I began.

"Why would that be rude? I'll answer you, once you answer that."

"I don't know, it might be an Irish thing, but I've noticed you could know someone around here for months before they ever got curious about what you do for a living."

"We're not like Americans in that respect, I'll give you that," Liam said with a nod. Anyway, I'm a musician. I used to be a teacher, but now I'm a full-time musician."

"What did you teach?"

"I taught children."

"Anything specific?"

"All subjects, really," he said. "I always wanted to be a teacher, ever since I was young. I did it for six years, but then the music started taking over, so I've put it on the long finger for now."

"Do you think you'll ever get back to it?" I asked.

"Mind you, that's a possibility, but I play out four or five nights a week, and I'm recording a record now. Then of course there's touring every now and again, so it keeps me pretty busy."

"Must be a wonderful way of life," I said. "It seems like such an accomplishment. I'm always so impressed by people who have taken a musical instrument and made it their own—you know, by people who can play in a way that only they can play. I have a brother like that."

"What does he play?"

"Guitar, but not for a living. He just plays."

"So, you must know a little bit about music," Liam stated.

"Yes, at least I think so. I think music is an intuitive language. People either speak it, or they don't. What I like best about music is for people who understand the language, very little else matters to the same degree. It's hard to put into words."

"I know," said Liam. "You really can't put it into words, but I think you've come close to capturing the point."

"It's freezing out here," I finally said, looking out toward the blackened sea. I couldn't actually see the water; I was only aware of a shrouding mist that permeated the air.

"It's a little cold, yah; I'll drive you home, then." He

stood up.

We walked back to the car surrounded by that feeling you have when you're first getting to know someone. It is consciousness in a way. Whether it's consciousness of a new presence, or self-consciousness is hard to say—probably it's a little of both.

Back to the main road we went, turning left, heading toward my home in Inverin. It's so dark between Spiddal and Inverin that I leaned forward in my seat, wanting to make sure I saw the driveway in time to notify Liam. "It's just here on the right," I said, pointing.

Liam pulled in the driveway and stopped the car. "I still have the cans," he said softly, letting the car continue to idle. Three thoughts raced through my mind: *First of all, it's late; secondly, if I point that out, I'll probably offend him; and third, what are the chances of ever seeing him again if I point out the time?* We looked at each other for an awkward moment.

"Would you like to come in?" I eventually asked. "We could sit out on the porch for a little while."

I hate situations like that. I tend to be my own worst enemy because I weigh everything to such an annoying degree. Rather than simply living in the moment and going with the flow, I analyze everything to death. I was thinking I didn't want Liam to think I made a habit of inviting strangers into my house. Then I was thinking what was worse, I just ran into him out of the blue, so it wasn't like this was a date. Did he think I was picking him up? I hoped not. Then it occurred to me that I don't know how things happen in Ireland, but given that, why would I alter my usual behavior just because I happened to be in Ireland? My mind continued to turn.

Liam followed me inside. I pulled open a drawer in the kitchen, looking for a bottle opener after I'd noticed of all the beer indigenous to Ireland, Liam had purchased Budweiser in longneck bottles. I took it as a sensitive gesture, as a way of making me feel at home, so to speak. The funny thing is, I've always thought Budweiser tastes like bad water compared to Irish beer. I came close to mentioning this until I got sidetracked, realizing the bottles were what Liam called cans. We each took a bottle and walked through the porch to the gray stone wall that lay at the bottom of the sloping front yard. The light from the porch was the only light in the area. It shone faintly behind us as we sat beneath a sky painted in follow-the-dot stars.

"I've sat on this wall before, Liam said, positioning himself to let his legs hang over.

"When?" I asked.

"Years ago, when I was younger. I used to cut the grass here."

"For my landlord, Mr. O'Flaherty?"

"Yes," he said quietly.

Somehow, I couldn't picture Liam mowing a yard. It just seemed inconsistent with everything about his refined, subtle manner.

"Small world," I said, "and now here you are years later, sitting on the same wall with a total stranger."

I could see him smiling in the dark. "Do you believe in things meant to be?"

"Sometimes," I said. "I guess what I really mean is yes, but not necessarily all the time. I think some things that happen to us are meant to be, and other things are of our own doing. Maybe circumstances evolve in our lives that are meant to be, but after that, the real question concerns what we're going to do with them."

"I see your point. Predestination versus free will. Where does God fit in?" he continued.

"Where do you think God fits in?" I turned the tables.

"First things first: do you believe in God? Are you a religious person?" Liam asked.

"This is getting awfully heavy, but yes," I said, "I believe in God. As far as any particular religion goes, sometimes I think I believe in everything. It's getting specific I have trouble with."

"I know," he said. "We can be taught one thing growing up, but it turns out it's not enough information. I like to read what some of the great minds have to say about the existence of God. Mind you, this is Catholic Ireland. I have to go outside for these things."

"What great minds?" I wanted to know.

"People like Plato or Aristotle or Einstein. I read a lot," he said.

"Was it Einstein who said time isn't necessarily linear?"

"T'was. Yeats was on about the same thing."

"Another great mind," I said.

"He was that. Yeats and his contemporaries were fascinated by the occult, you know."

"Contemporaries like whom?"

"People like John Synge and Lady Augusta Gregory—the writers and actors around him in Ireland while he was making his name. They were all here together, inspiring each other to be better artists."

"So, when you say the occult, exactly what are you talking about?" I asked.

"Actually, Yeats was exploring mysticism, but when I said occult, I meant the spiritual side of things. Exploring other dimensions, like."

"Sooner or later, any intelligent human being does that, don't you think?"

"Well look at us now!" Liam said.

"We flatter ourselves," I added.

"We do indeed, but I think it all has to do plain and simply with a universal search for the truth. Each of us has our own individual way with the truth, you know. No one else can name it for us, or give us the rules because they're our own."

"Well said," I noted, and I meant it.

We sat on the wall for more than an hour talking about anything that entered our minds. I kept thinking Liam was deep. He seemed pensive and opinionated. He had the soul of an artist and seemed to be seeking a like mind, as if he were striving to be understood. *This isn't someone who takes things on the chin,* I thought. I had the impression he was trying to sort things out, as if he were trying to find his way in the scheme of things by trying mysteries on for size to see if they fit.

It was three in the morning when I stood up on the wall and said I should be going. It can be uncomfortable to be the one to make that call, and when I did, it seemed Liam grew skittish, as if I'd said he'd overstayed his welcome. He moved inside quickly, scooped up his keys from the kitchen counter and then turned abruptly, heading hastily for the door. I only had time to say I hoped to see him play sometime, then he was gone like a rocket into the night.

"See you at the gig sometime," he called over his shoulder before he closed the porch door. I stood staring out the window with confusion, wondering if I had inadvertently put Liam off, and if I had, exactly how had that happened?

Chapter Four

Although I fought my confusion at nagging intervals, I didn't have a lot of time to worry about Liam because the following week was to be the Galway Music Centre's first acoustic showcase at a wildly popular venue on High Street called the Kings Head, and the stakes of our fledgling reputation were too high to squander my energy elsewhere. For the preceding month, we'd scrambled by calling in every resource we had to produce the show; we had to rush because we wanted to seize the opportunity of a surprise cancellation, as there wouldn't be another opening for months to come.

After we booked the room, we agreed upon five local musicians we thought were worthy of showcasing in Galway, and approached each one with the offer of public exposure as opposed to pay, which I thought might be a negligible proposition, yet all of them eagerly complied. We put Darren in charge of lighting and sound, Declan as master of ceremonies, Shannon as keeper of the door, and I was the point person for all the musicians, as in any questions or concerns they had went through me. Although it had been a hectic month, it was devoid of any formalities I expected; business in Galway, it turned out, could be done with no contracts to sign, only promises to keep on a friendly handshake.

I discovered it was easy enough to get word around Galway. For starters, there was the *Galway Advertiser,* which came out every Thursday. For only eight euros, one could place an ad in the widely circulated newspaper, which could be found in every shop, on every corner, and with every newsagent in town. In promoting the Centre's show, we utilized the *Advertiser* as well as a young man from Athenry by the name of Adrian Johnson, who was an enthusiastic lad who only wanted to be a part of the Centre. Adrian didn't care what he did, and although he was the only one of us not earning a wage, he arrived at the Centre each day ready for action as if his life depended on it.

Adrian liked the feel of the place, he liked the business we were involved in, he liked considering himself an integral part of it all, and he really liked hanging around basking in his own importance. Each day, Adrian would bang through the Centre's wooden door, stand with his hands on his hips looking up to the loft and shout, "How's the form?" and each time he did, Shannon and I exchanged suppressed laughs because it was one of the many Irish expressions that just tickled our American sensibilities.

It was Adrian who plastered every available inch of wall space in Galway City with posters announcing our show. The posters went everywhere Adrian did because he was on a mission. "I'm going into town!" Adrian would proclaim, fueled by the fire of official business, even though "town" was only about a two-minute stride away. Out the door he would roar, posters clamped against his chest, bifocal glasses framing gray-green eyes beneath excessively curly, sandy-brown hair that swayed with his earnest momentum.

Declan was intolerant of Adrian and never bothered to hide the fact he thought Adrian was a ne'er do well, a hanger-on, someone who was in his jurisdictional space. He would scowl at Adrian and throw his energy around in an unmistakable whirling huff as if Adrian was in the way, but Shannon and I adored Adrian. We made up for Declan by creating chores for him to do; we explained things to him, sent him out on errands, and solicited his advice even though it was never required. For all of his significance or lack thereof, within the Galway Music Centre, Adrian Johnson was both the most polarizing and the most discussed.

A mid-afternoon reprieve on the day of the showcase found Shannon and me sitting outside with Adrian on the ledge that jutted from the Centre's courtyard wall as I recounted the story of meeting Liam Hennessey. I considered the fact that I had the insight of a levelheaded American and a local Irish lad at my avail. I thought I should take advantage of the opportunity, so I spilled the facts. Surely there was something about Liam I missed that night. I thought maybe between the two of them, I could get to the bottom of his weird behavior. Adrian's immediate response was, "He must be over the moon over you."

"How in the world did you get that?" I was completely baffled.

"He drove you home," he stated simply.

"And he came in," Shannon added.

"I know, but then he flipped out and ran out the door never mentioning seeing me again. 'See you at the gig sometime' was all he said, like I'm supposed to just show up some night and hang around worshiping at the altar of his talent."

"I think he wants to see if you're interested," Adrian went on.

"So why doesn't he ask?"

"He's not going to ask." Shannon looked at me as if it were obvious. "They don't do that here. It would be too direct."

"He'll probably have to see you once or twice more," Adrian concluded. "A lad has to be sure."

"I don't know how that's going to happen unless I bump into him on the street," I said. "And I'm not just going to show up at a gig, what would be the point? Those guys don't take a break all night. They only have extended pauses and even then, they don't take them together because the music never stops. All I'd be able to do is show up and watch him."

"You'll bump into him on the street then," Adrian said. "This is Galway."

"Speaking of streets, I should go to the Kings Head and tell Paul the sound check will be tonight at six thirty," I said. "Adrian, you want to come?"

"Sure, maybe we'll run into Prince Charming."

"If we do, act like you don't know me. I wouldn't want him to think I was hanging around with the likes of you," I joked.

"Very funny, Hailey, and me just wanting to be by your side," he said. Shannon looked at me out of the corner of her eye and gave me a wink.

We walked up the central thoroughfare of Shop Street together, navigating through a mixed throng of locals, tourists, college students, and country dwellers in from the rural fields to the worldliness of Galway City. Through dingy pub windows coated to a gray film from decades of cigarette smoke and smoldering turf fires, publicans cranked levers of Guinness on draught, lining up pint glasses on the bar to stabilize the pungent, dark porter until it magically separated the body from its frothy head, thick as marshmallow. Adrian buzzed nonstop in anticipation of the show until he got a better plan out of nowhere and bounced off on his merry way with a wave and a smile.

I continued toward the Kings Head, weaving through the discordant crowd and realized with startling attunement that I was listening to the sounds of an accordion wafting through the air from some unnamed quarter. My first thought was of Liam. I turned around, eyes scanning, half expecting to see him, thinking for all I knew, he could be one of the many musicians who busk on the streets of Galway. When I steadied my gaze, I brought Kieran Murphy into focus; he was walking three people deep behind me. His head was turned to the side and he walked quickly with hunched shoulders against the bracing wind. I hadn't seen Kieran since that night in Hughes. Without thinking of what to say, I let him catch up to me, and then I fell in line with his gait.

Startled, he looked at me and immediately began apologizing. He talked so fast I could barely understand the words spilling forth, but I could make out he'd been embarrassed the next day, even though he couldn't recall exactly why. Because he looked so ashamed, I knew the only kind thing to do was give him the time to unburden himself, so I waited through his apology, and then let him off the hook.

"While I was playing in the session that night, Liam's brother looked over at the two of you and said, 'It looks like Liam is stealing your girl.'"

"He said that?" I wanted to hear more.

"He did."

"What did you say?"

"I said, 'Nobody can compete with Liam.'"

"It was nice meeting Liam, so since it was you who introduced us, I guess I'll have to forgive you," I said, trying to diffuse the situation. I knew whatever I said to Kieran would eventually get back to Liam, which is exactly why I made a point of saying it was nice meeting him. Liam and Kieran both lived in the same area of Inverin, and paths cross often there—that, and people talk.

"So, I guess Liam fancies you," Kieran said.

"I don't know about that, Kieran, you never know," I said.

The one thing I did know is there's always a period of uncertainty that comes into play upon meeting someone who interests you. It must be inherent in attraction, for I've never met anybody who hasn't experienced it, it's just a question of to what degree they're going to admit it. Waiting for someone to make the first move can be draining: you question what your role should be, what actions are appropriate, what would be off-putting, what would translate into indifference, and what would give encouragement. It's a wonder anything ever gets off the ground while you're busy soldiering on, acting as if none of it is happening.

I returned to the Kings Head that night just in time for the sound check, then milled around afterward until the show began at nine. It was easy to while away the time because there is always something happening beneath the roof of the rambling, historic pub on the High Street. Throughout the decades, the Kings Head has been renovated repeatedly, but the feeling inside is musty and old. Its floors are wooden and its interior walls are gray stone just like the stone you find throughout rural Ireland. Heavy wrought-iron chandeliers hang from the ceiling lit from bulbs like stationary candle flames. Attached to various walls or hanging from the ceiling are unusual antiquities: a wooden Celtic harp, a copper kettle, a whale-oil lantern. The three floors are connected by plank-and-iron staircases with the second floor exposed so that you can look down from the third floor unobstructed.

Every once in a while, I watched the third-floor door

thinking maybe Liam would recall my mention of the show and decide to put in an appearance. I wandered into the hallway where Shannon was guarding the stairs. She'd pulled a table from the bar area to the foot of the stairs, and sat granting admission for a fee of eight euros. Her auburn hair was swept into a conservative bun, and she wore a teal silk shirt under a black blazer with matching trousers.

"How many people are here?" I asked.

Shannon glanced down at her clipboard. "So far, sixty."

"Do you want to switch places so you can watch for a while?" I asked, since the show was in full swing.

"I'm all right," she said in that succinct manner of hers.

A pint of Guinness was before her, and Darren sat draping his long, athletic body on a chair at her side. The two looked content to stay there in the company of each other all night, so I walked back through the double doors of the music room and stood watching a singer named Ruth Dillon begin her set when Declan appeared beside me. Shouting above the music, he screamed into my ear, "I'm not going to stand on stage and announce anymore. That's it."

"That's it?" I exclaimed. "Why not?" *Surely he's kidding,* I thought.

"I don't like standing up there in front of everyone. It makes me nervous."

"Come on, Declan, you can't do that," I said, not taking him seriously. "You're the face of the Music Centre. You're the guy who started the place; you're supposed to be the emcee. We talked about this."

"I'm not going to do it, and there it is," he huffed, his mouth clamped to a straight line.

Suddenly it hit me he was serious. I glared at Declan, who remained with his arms folded across his chest and his feet firmly planted. I couldn't decide if I was flabbergasted or annoyed. *This is a fine time for Declan to decide to change the plan,* I thought. I listened as Ruth Dillon moved through her second song on stage, thinking she had two more songs before I had to figure out what to do. I opened the doors to the hallway and stood once again before Shannon and Darren.

"Guess what," I said. "Declan says he's not going to emcee anymore."

"You're kidding," said Shannon, but there was no note of surprise in her voice.

"Brilliant," said Darren. The three of us looked at each other, speechless.

"Where's Adrian?" I finally asked.

"You can forget that," Darren said, looking at me levelly.

I stood a moment longer until Shannon said, "Hailey, you have to do it."

There was no way around it, Shannon was right, somebody had to rise to the occasion. I finished out the introductions of each musician because we were all in it now. I stood on the stage in front of an all-Irish audience, speaking in a Southern accent no amount of years spent elsewhere could budge and hoped the people before me understood what I was saying. I kept thinking the musicians on stage were playing free of charge and deserved the respect. It was that, and we had to save face for the Centre.

After the show, Shannon held open the double doors for Darren as he angled the table she'd been using back to the room on the third floor. She carried an aluminum strongbox that held the money we'd made, and put its key in her pocket.

"Success," she said, walking over to me.

"If you're willing to overlook Declan's behavior, success," I said, looking around for the switch to the stage lights.

"No, seriously, we made a profit after expenses. Where is he?" she said. "By the way, we're going to have to overlook his behavior, but you already know that."

"Yah, I do know that. Declan's downstairs at the bar having a pint with Paul Greeley."

We found Declan and Paul on the first floor surrounded by four other Greeley's, all the spitting image of each other with their black hair and blue eyes. The entire Greeley family worked at the Kings Head and could be found in any capacity from bouncer to short-order cook. Paul scratched back his barstool when he saw us coming and gave us his big toothy smile.

"Well now, 'tis themselves, the Americans who can teach us a thing or two about putting on a show. Give us a hand here, Declan, get these girls a pint. Darren, are you well?" he said, extending his hand to Darren.

"I'm all right, mate," Darren answered. "Did you see any of the show?" Darren pulled out the chair next to Paul and sat down, holding up his index finger to the bartender, who started pouring a Guinness without being asked.

"I did, yah, it was gorgeous. Youse can all come back here any time."

"That's what meself and Paul were just saying, we can make this a regular thing," Declan said. "Hailey, half-pint or full?"

"Half," I said, as Shannon nodded. Declan turned toward the bartender, putting his hands in a t-stop and in a short moment, two half-pints were placed before us as the bartender smiled and said, "Now." I shot a glance at

Shannon, who couldn't resist the urge to mouth "there." Her tendency to translate Irish idioms had become a standing joke that followed us wherever we went.

"Great news, we'd love to make this a regular thing," Shannon said to Paul.

"Right, then, we will, so," Paul said as Declan pulled out his wallet. "Ah, no, on me," Paul said with a wave of his hand.

At one in the morning, Shannon, Darren, Declan and I left the Kings Head. Always acting as a unit, the three of them walked me to the hackney office across the street from Taylor's Pub so I could get a lift out to Inverin. There wasn't a soul on the misty, gray streets and our footsteps echoed and ricocheted off the vacant buildings lining the damp street. Declan reached in his pocket and handed me money for the fare, shaking his head when I tried to protest.

"Sorry, Hailey," Declan began. I didn't have to ask what he meant as I watched his eyes dart around as if trying to decide where to land before I finally caught his gaze.

"It's okay, we got it done," I said. Declan lifted his pocket watch from its chain then secured it in his pocket, standing up to his full authority and clearing his throat. "Tell youse what, let's open tomorrow at noon," he said to all of our agreement.

It wasn't often I had cause to make the journey from Galway to Inverin by hackney at night, but when I did, it was always a rather eerie experience. The total darkness on the two-lane coast road, the way the moon illuminated the sea in hues of black, cobalt blue, and silver, the lonesome stretches of treeless landscape along the side of the road, and the complete absence of sound made the journey surreal as I watched the night for signposts guiding me home. The ride would be a gradual change of consciousness as I left the activity of Galway behind and crept stealthily into the bleak solitude of Inverin. There would be conversation with the hackney driver from start to finish. It would be a stranger and me traveling together with the same destination, and in that singular instance, we shared something in common. Any conversation would be enlightening as I listened to the driver, conscious of his dialect, his peculiar accent, and the unique phrasing of his words.

On this night, the hackney driver was a thirty-five-year-old local named Michael Connolly. At one time, he'd lived in the US for two years and reported without hesitation, "That was enough for me!" On the state of California and the city of Los Angeles he said, "My idea of heaven would be Ireland with Los Angeles weather; my idea of hell would be Los Angeles with Irish weather." On Americans in general, he glanced over at me shyly and said, "Not very subtle now, are they?"

After a lull in the conversation, as we listened to the Irish traditional music playing on the radio, Michael Connolly continued, "All the best traditional musicians come from the west of Ireland, don'tcha know. You've heard of the Hennesseys, have you?

"Once or twice," I said, thinking, *loose lips sink ships, and with my luck, this guy probably lives next door to Liam.*

Chapter Five

It's funny how things come around if you allow them, as in; it's funny how things come around if you don't get in your own way and screw everything up. On a clear, warm sunny Tuesday morning, I walked down Shop Street thinking about the five minute's worth of accordion music I'd just heard over the radio on the bus into Galway. *Liam,* I thought. *Liam the box player. This is a coincidence, and I'm a big believer in coincidence. Maybe something's up—I better keep my eyes open just in case this is a sign.* I started over O'Brien's bridge and headed to the Centre.

"Hi, Hailey," a voice in front of me said. Holding my arm up to block the sunlight, I made out the face of Patrick.

"Hi, Patrick," I said, caught unaware.

"Where you going?" He looked down at me with a gripping stare.

"Just into work," I said.

"Where's that?" He leaned an elbow on the bridge as if he had all the time in the world.

"The Galway Music Centre on New Road," I said. "Have you ever heard of it?"

"No, never have. What do you do there?"

"We're working with local musicians, trying to help organize their careers." I explained briefly, wondering if he was truly interested, or just making conversation.

"My brother Steve and I are in Galway today trying to line up a few gigs. Maybe we'll call out when we're through this afternoon," Patrick said.

"You're a musician?" I asked. Somehow, I couldn't

picture it. Patrick looked more like a sailor of the seven seas than a musician, but I've been fooled by appearances before.

"My whole family plays. We're all living out in Spiddal, playing music. Have been for the past two years," he said.

"What do you play?"

"Fiddle," he said.

I still couldn't picture it but decided to take his word for it anyway.

"Well, all right, you should come by the Centre then," I said. "We'll be there until the end of the day."

"You'll be there until the six-o'clock bus," Patrick said, winking and turning to go.

Some people are always saying they're going to do something, and you never know if they're actually going to follow through, but at four o'clock that afternoon, into the courtyard of the Music Centre strolled Patrick and his brother Steve. I introduced them to Shannon, Darren and Adrian as if I knew them better than I did and just kind of stood there pointlessly while they leisurely paced around, looking things over.

"So," Patrick said, turning to me and getting down to business, "do you go out in Inverin a lot?"

"Not a lot," I said, "I haven't been in Ireland that long. I don't know that many people in Inverin, they're mostly here in Galway, so I really don't go out very much in Inverin."

"You know Liam." Patrick stared directly at me.

Patrick is probably the frankest guy I will ever meet; what's he doing—interrogating me? I wondered.

"Liam's a really nice guy," I volunteered for the record, because I knew one was being kept.

"Liam's a very accomplished musician," Patrick said,

championing the cause. "He's come with us to New Zealand twice as a guest musician, people love him there."

"Cool," I said, for lack of anything better to say.

"You should come out and see Liam play," Patrick continued. While he kept staring at me, I kept wondering what he knew, for example: did he know the last time I saw Liam he shot out of my house like the hounds of hell were on his heels?

"Maybe I will," I said. It was obvious Patrick was on a quest.

"Liam would be glad to see you if you did," he stated unequivocally.

I turned toward Shannon with as much casualness as I could feign. "Do you remember me telling you about meeting Prince Charming in Spiddal?" I asked.

Shannon nodded.

"Patrick's a good friend of his," I added. Shannon smiled at Patrick, registering the information.

"We'll be playing in Spiddal this Saturday night. You should come out. Liam will be there," Patrick said.

"I will if Shannon and Darren will come with me," I said, looking at Shannon.

"Right, so we'll see you there," Patrick concluded.

"All right. Thanks for stopping in," I said.

"Nice to meet you," Shannon, Darren, and Adrian said in overlapping unison as Patrick and Steve sailed away.

"Good one, Hailey. He's going to tell Liam you called him Prince Charming," Shannon said, the second they were out of earshot.

"Exactly," I said. "He's on his way now."

Two nights later, I sat in the dim light of my living room reading a book. I heard the sliding glass door whisk open, then heavily shut with a thud followed by an immediate rap on the living room door. When I opened it, Liam stood there looking like a deer caught in headlights, holding a leather-bound book in his hand.

"Hi, Liam." I smiled broadly. We stood there awkwardly for what seemed like all of eternity until he finally spoke.

"I've just come 'round to bring you a book, it's a collection of English essays. You did say you like to read."

"Oh, yes, thank you, do you want to come in?" I opened the door a little wider. Liam stepped in. He seemed so nervous I half expected him to hand me the book then turn around and run. He followed me out onto the porch and sat down across from me. Eventually his long, lithe body started to relax. He brought up the subject of the night we met in Hughes, and said he found it a curiosity I had come with Kieran. "He has quite a reputation for imposing himself upon women," Liam said pointedly.

"I wasn't actually with him," I explained, "Leigh and I just walked across the street with Kieran."

"When I saw Kieran walk out of Hughes behind you, I thought I'd better follow to make sure you weren't attacked," Liam said.

I couldn't help but laugh. "Pleasant thought, I really would have been fine, but thank you for doing that."

"I've been reading Lord Byron since you mentioned you liked him," Liam said.

This must be his veiled way of letting me know he's been thinking of me. It's a strenuous exercise trying to read between the lines with this guy, I thought.

I studied Liam as he spoke and kept thinking how well-mannered and poised he was. He was impressively articulate, then suddenly he'd turn around and speak like one of the local Irish lads using words like "anyway" too often, and ending each question with the words, "Is it?"

"So, you're here alone tonight, is it?" Liam asked.

"I am," I confirmed.

As it was a Thursday night, Liam was scheduled to play at the Lisheen in Galway. He explained to me that a few of the local "trad" musicians had standing gigs at some of the pubs in Galway during the tourist season, and he'd been doing it for years.

"Do you want to come with me tonight?" he asked tentatively. "I should be leaving soon. I'm on at ten."

We drove the coast road through the sleepy towns of Spiddal, Barna, Furbo, and Salt Hill, the sea to our right all the while until we finally touched down in Galway. Parking on the left side of the road, we crossed the street and entered the Lisheen, where Liam stationed me in the center of the room before making his way through the crowd to the stage.

I love to watch professional musicians as they prepare to perform. There's something so regal about them. I love the way they carry their instrument as if it were something sacred, and I admire the command they have of all space on stage where everything is arranged to an effectual degree in their own private jurisdiction. It is serious business, this business of setting up, and it is spellbinding to watch, like a mystifying, choreographed dance whose inception is just as much a part of the performance as everything that follows.

I stood thinking it's not so bad standing alone in a crowd when you've come with someone who's on stage. It gives you the opportunity to watch the musician, to study him silently from a distance without being studied yourself, although once or twice Liam spied me in the crowd and gave me an inclusive smile.

The thing about Irish traditional music is the more you listen to it, the more complicated it becomes. It's hard for the layman to decipher which instrument leads, but the musicians stay connected by a type of active listening to a language whose individual parts coalesce in a tightly woven tapestry of unified sound. I noticed Liam had the same transported look in his eyes as he had the first time I saw him play. It was as if the music moved through him, and there's a big difference between simply playing an instrument and opening yourself up as a channel so it can move through you. He played with total disregard to the number of people in the room: there could have been two, or there could have been two thousand. It didn't seem to affect his reverential posture whatsoever.

There are many pubs in Ireland where traditional music is played, but it is only incidental ambience in the background of a noisy pub without the intention of being a focal point. That isn't the way it was at the Lisheen. The people at the Lisheen had come specifically to see these three men play, and after they stopped, the crowd filed up to them waiting to talk, wanting to praise. Being courteous and accommodating after a gig is technically the end of the performance for the Irish traditional player, and I watched Liam humbly receive his admirers like a prince holding court. Shortly thereafter, he wound his way to my side and asked if I was ready to leave.

Back on the wall in front of my house, Liam and I sat watching the stars. It was easier this time because all of the guesswork had been taken out of things. The ambiguity of the situation had lessened by the simple act of Liam returning to see me, and we talked comfortably of things that interested him: spiritual issues, the nature of dreams, classical music, and imported red wines. Our conversation was partly philosophical, and partly a means of assessing each other, for it was clear he wanted to know me, and he wanted for me to know him. I watched him in the dark, thinking this is the most poetic creature I've ever seen. With his deliberate yet gentle mannerisms and his dark good looks, I kept thinking if he only had a black woolen cape, he'd look just like the description of Heathcliff in *Wuthering Heights.* The hours flew by, and this time I remained where I was until Liam volunteered it was time for him to leave; it was two thirty in the morning.

"When will I see you again?" he asked.

Being grateful for being asked in such a subtle manner, I replied, "Whenever you would like."

"I'll come again very soon," he said.

Chapter Six

Upstairs at the Centre, Declan called a meeting to order. Shannon, Darren, Adrian, and I circled around him, waiting for him to get to the point.

"Right," he began. "It seems folks are talking about the Centre saying we don't support Irish musicians."

"What do you mean by folks?" Darren interrupted.

"Just folks are talking," Declan said quickly. "It's about the showcase." In a complete personality role reversal for Shannon and Declan, Declan spoke cryptically until Shannon asked him to just get to the point.

"We shouldn't have put Leigh McDonough on stage because she's not Irish, nor is Brian Keeney," Declan said vehemently.

"But the entire point of the showcase was to put the best of Galway on stage," Shannon said.

"They're not Irish," Declan said hotly. "The Centre is about Irish music."

"I thought the Centre is all about the musicians in Galway," I said, looking at Declan.

"It is about the musicians in Galway, but they're supposed to be Irish," he said.

"But if this is what's happening in Galway right now, if the musicians actually live here in town, then in a sense, they're Irish musicians or at the least, musicians in Ireland," Darren qualified.

"It's making us look bad," Declan said definitively. "I'm getting away from the plan I had for the Centre."

"Declan, you didn't have a specific plan for the Centre," Shannon reminded him. "The idea was to provide Galway with what was missing in the way of services for local musicians; we're learning what's needed as we go along."

"He's just upset because people are talking about him," Darren cut to the chase.

Suddenly, the door opened downstairs, and in with the wind blew Liam Hennessey. Declan leaned over the railing looking down at him.

"It's Prince Charming," he said, as he turned back to me. I walked to the landing at the top of the stairs and looked down for myself. Sure enough, there he was. I descended the stairs slowly, nervous with the surprise of his unplanned appearance.

"Hi, Liam," I managed to say.

"Hi," he said, all black hair and brown eyes shining. "I'm just in town for the afternoon. Will you be needing a lift back later?"

"Yes," I said, "but not until around five or so."

"That's grand, that's just when I'll be leaving myself."

"Do you want to come back then? Do you want me to show you around now? There's not much to see, but I could show you around if you'd like," I said.

"I'd rather meet you at Taaffes later. You do know where Taaffes is, yah?"

"Yah," I said.

"Right, I'll be looking for you there at five, then."

"All right, see you then," I said.

With that, he was gone. I began to walk back up the stairs.

"So," Declan began walking toward me, his eyebrows mischievously raised with the sport of ridicule spreading over his face.

"Declan, don't start," I said, rejoining the group.

Taaffes is a hallmark in Galway. It is a pub as old as the streets themselves with no fanfare outside, just a small tinted rectangular window and a discreet wooden door heralding a room that is dark as a tomb inside no matter the time of day.

I walked into Taaffes a few minutes after five and saw Liam sitting at the bar talking to the bartender. I sat down on the stool beside him and accepted the half-pint of Guinness the bartender placed before me as if he read my mind.

"Well, now I've seen where you work," Liam said.

"You have." I nodded. "Thanks for coming by."

"Glad to do it. My brother Anthony will be here in a minute. He and his friend Eamon are playing here tonight."

"Anthony plays guitar, right?" I asked. "I think I saw him playing guitar in Hughes, didn't I?"

"He does. He sings as well, not very well, mind you, but he tries."

"So, what's he sing?" I asked.

"Songs from American songwriters mostly, people like James Taylor and John Denver," he said.

It's amazing the things that make it over here, I thought. *I don't know anybody who takes John Denver seriously in America.*

"Do you have any other brothers besides Anthony?" I asked.

"No, but I have a sister," he said. "People say we look exactly alike."

"What's her name?" I asked, thinking if she looked anything like Liam, she must be absolutely beautiful.

"Nula," he said.

"Named after your mother or grandmother?"

"My grandmother," he said.

"On your mother's side?" I asked.

"Yes, did I tell you that before?"

"I don't think so."

"Then how did you know?"

"I didn't; I was just guessing," I said. Since most names in Ireland are family names, it wasn't that big of a stretch.

"So, you're a psychic then!"

"I'm not a psychic, Liam. Please," I said.

Liam's brother came bursting into the pub and headed straight for us, coming to a smiling stop and looking me in the eyes as Liam turned to me saying, "You remember Anthony, yah?"

Anthony stood looking me over with eyes suggesting he had all the facts. He was older than Liam, and was his complete physical opposite. Where Liam was dark, Anthony was light; where Liam looked mysterious and withdrawn, Anthony had a wide-open freckled face, big blue eyes and an eager manner. "Hiya," Anthony sang, beaming at me.

"Hi, Anthony," I said, as if I knew him. "Does anyone ever call you Tony?"

"Ah, good question from an American," he said, "I've heard that one before. We don't pronounce the letter *H* over here. Naw, I'm not a Tony, just an An-Tony."

"Very good, I got it. What time are you on tonight?"

"Not until eight," he said. "We're just here to set up. If you miss it, you won't be missing much from me; Liam's the real singer in the family."

Surprised, I looked at Liam. "You sing?" I asked.

"I don't," he said quickly. "At least not in public."

"He should sing in public, but he never will," Anthony sang his brother's praise.

"All right, if you were to sing, what would you sing?

70

What kind of music do you listen to?"

"He likes Sting and Chris De Burgh. He has all of Chris De Burgh's records," Anthony answered for him. "You're familiar with Chris De Burgh, yah? 'The Lady in Red?' Liam loves that song."

"I know the song," I said.

"Chris De Burgh is Irish, did you know that?"

"No, I had no idea," I said.

"Oh yah, and Liam can sing just like him," Jimmy said. "You should hear him."

Liam seemed embarrassed during this exchange while his brother did the talking for him. "Liam is known all over Ireland as one of the best box players around, but the truth is he's good at everything: he composes, arranges, sings and teaches—he can do everything and do it well," Anthony said, just as a stout young man wearing a waxed jacket joined us. "You ready?" Anthony turned to the young man.

"I am, yah."

"This is Hailey; she's an American." Anthony clapped a proprietary hand on my shoulder. "This is Eamon," he said. Eamon made no pretense of hiding his newcomer's once-over.

"Let's do this," Anthony directed, and the two retreated to set up the stage.

"Are you and Anthony close?" I turned to Liam.

"Not really. I guess we're about as close as I am to anyone," he answered vaguely.

I don't know why, but I thought Liam's quick response was kind of odd, or maybe it was just telling. You have to watch people when you're first getting to know them because they send out clues when you least expect it, and you'd be doing very well to pay attention. I wondered if this was an insight into Liam's character.

Was he telling me he'd never had the desire to be close to anyone? Was he indicating he wasn't capable of closeness? What was he doing sitting here with me if that were the case? I decided to keep an eye on it and just let time tell.

What time told in the days and nights that followed was that Liam Hennessey was on the case and everything ran together in one exhaustive blur. Two weeks after Liam appeared at the Centre, I sat in my porch writing in my journal, documenting how much had evolved in such a short amount of time, feeling as though I'd been thrust into a new set of circumstances from the singular event of Liam's entrance in my life. At some point, I began to expect the sound of my sliding glass door sweeping heavily aside, followed by a knock on my living room door. I never knew when it would come, but I began to listen for it right around the time the sun set.

Sometimes Liam would have a plan in mind, other times he just came to sit and talk. I never knew which it was going to be, and it didn't much matter; I was just happy to have him around. Some nights, we walked through the fields to the sea, sitting down in that place at the land's end where two gigantic boulders sat side by side on an elevated patch hovering over the Atlantic. The first time I took him there, Liam turned to me and said, "You discovered this place on your own, yah? Is this an initiation?" Humoring him, I assured him that it was.

"It's not just anybody I would take here," I said, much to his approval.

"Ah, then, this is your way of chasing new romance!"

I stopped and considered. The thing about new romance is there's an unbalancing undercurrent in its heated thrall. You're never quite sure where you stand in the other's eyes until the subject is broached or some overt gesture is made. It is ambiguous guesswork until then; the air is thick with it. Maybe I was chasing new romance, but I wasn't sure what I was getting in return.

"How long am I going to have to pursue you until you start pursuing me back?" Liam said unexpectedly, and with that, he leaned over and kissed me for the first time, turning the tides from friendship to romance.

On a warm, windy night, Liam arrived at my door carrying a bottle of red wine and a stack of CDs. He put them on the kitchen counter, turned to me and said, "Right then, it's time to educate you if you're not already familiar with Mozart, Bach, Schubert, Brahms and Beethoven. These are for you to keep; I have a backup collection at home," he said, walking to the kitchen drawer to find a bottle opener while he watched for my response. He poured the wine, pressed play on the stereo, and spent the following four hours introducing me to his favorite composers as if he knew them all personally.

I never would have assumed any of this from an Irish traditional musician, but it was becoming increasingly apparent Liam was so much more. He had a true understanding of all music genres and listened with the focused attention most people lend to the task of reading a book. He explained the inherent nuances within the movements enthusiastically, then paused and listened as if he were hearing them for the first time. It is one thing to listen to music, but Liam actually experienced it as if he were aligned to some unnamed dimension. Watching him, I couldn't help but be affected. It was a lot like being taught poetry from a true poet, and we stayed captive within the music until I finally looked at the clock's late hour.

"Time moves quickly in this room," Liam said,

getting up to leave. "Will you come with me to Clifden tomorrow night? I'm going to be a guest musician in a music festival."

"I'd love to," I said, walking him to the door.

We stopped in the doorway that joined the living room and the porch: me on the side of the living room and Liam a deep step below me on the porch. From this position, we were the same height and when we kissed and embraced, it felt as if we were connected in a hold culled from the intimacy we'd acquired from the long hours spent in each other's company. We were growing used to each other; there had been so many nights like this that parting was starting to seem like an interruption.

"I'll come collect you tomorrow at half six," he said.

"I'll be here," I said, releasing his embrace and closing the door behind him.

Chapter Seven

The distance between Inverin and Clifden is approximately sixty kilometers. It's a visually inspiring hour-long ride through undulating midlands with grass as soft as velvet, gray stone walls that split the landscape, and bubbling intermittent streams as you glide along a two-lane road that cuts through a terrain devoid of street markers, stop signs, or any other indication the area has been previously trodden. There is little suggestion of civilization anywhere in sight and it is a quiet, unobstructed journey through the heart of Connemara with nothing in store, save for the destination of Clifden.

Driving into Clifden, one is abruptly thrust into the center of a thriving village that hosts an annual, three-day music festival wherein every pub door is invitingly open with signs outside announcing which Irish traditional musicians will be playing within the standing-room-only venues. A rudimentary chalkboard sat on the sidewalk outside of Mannion's Pub with "Welcome Liam Hennessey" sprawled across in large, eye-catching cursive.

I followed Liam into the middle of a waiting crowd, which parted ceremoniously as he made his way to the old man seated against the wall across from the bar. Wind-tossed and toothless, the man sat on a battered wooden chair, tuning a fiddle and nodding his greeting while Liam opened his accordion case and settled in beside him. When a flute player joined them, the crowd fell into an anticipatory hush, ready for the music to begin. I stationed myself in front of the bar, minding my own business, but that soon became short-lived.

"Are you here with Liam?" asked a middle-aged man who was standing too close to me.

"Yes." I took a step back.

"She's here with Liam," the man announced, turning to the man beside him.

"Ah," the second man gasped, "she is, so!"

"Where did you get that blond hair on your head?" The first man eyed me.

"I brought it with me from America," I said.

"She's from America!" The man turned to the other man, his eyes opened wide.

"America indeed!" The second man drew in his breath.

"All I want in the world is for me brother to come in and see me standing here talking to you," said the first man. "I wouldn't care if a pooka came for me after that. Will you have a pint? Get her a pint, Tom," he directed.

"Tom, make that a half-pint," I said, trying not to laugh. I looked over at an obviously amused Liam, who smiled and winked as if to say he knew what was happening.

I looked toward the door and noticed an unusually small woman walking in with what appeared to be members of her family due to their similarity in stature. I'd met her in Galway before: she was a musician named Deanna Rader who played guitar and sang anything from Irish traditional music to her own compositions. I'd heard her sing in her low, husky voice a few times before, and because she was a friend of Declan's, I'd exchanged pleasantries with her a few times as well. From the looks of things, she was in Mannion's with her father and two sisters. She came smiling to my side instantly.

"Well then, you've made your way out here now, have you?" She looked up at me.

"I came here with Liam," I said, grateful to know someone in the crowd.

"I knew you must have. So, it's the two of you now, is it?"

"Well, I don't know if I'd put it that way," I said, diverting the implication. I couldn't recall if I'd seen Deanna while I was out with Liam, or if she asked this because she'd heard people talking.

"You're a long way from home yourself," I said. "Is this festival a big deal?"

"Oh God, yes. People look forward every year. Luckily my parents live in Letterfrack, just up the road. I've been spending the last couple of nights with them. We've all come 'round tonight for the craic."

"Well, it's nice to know someone here," I said.

"My sister came out to sing tonight. Would you mind asking Liam if she could give us a song?"

"Sure," I said. "I'll ask him when they take a break."

"They probably won't do that, so you'd be waiting for ages," Deanna said. "You'll just have to lean over and ask, like."

"When?" I asked.

"How about now?" she said.

"Right now?"

"If it wouldn't be too much trouble," she smiled sweetly.

I looked over at the musicians, who were in full swing. There was no way I was going to butt in, even though Deanna kept standing there looking up at me expectantly. Just then, a man at the bar stepped forward enthusiastically. He leaned into the musicians circle, grabbed Liam by the arm, and shouted loudly, "The young lady here wants to give us a song." With that, the music came to a screeching halt, and a whirlwind of preparation commenced. Liam leaned over and whispered to the two musicians beside him, instruments were set down, a microphone was raised, a path spontaneously cleared, and into the arena stepped Deanna's sister. It was like the infamous scene of Marilyn Monroe singing "Happy Birthday" to President Kennedy.

There was a hush in the room as all eyes riveted upon the girl. She stood all of five foot two, but within that minuscule framework there was a lot going on: thick, raven hair fell in loose waves across her forehead and down her back. Large green oval eyes slanted and squinted catlike beneath thick, dark lashes. Turn by turn, her eyes focused and held one man in the room after another. She stood with her right hand on her hip and her voluptuous weight shifted to the left. With great histrionics, she crooned out a song in the Irish language I'd never heard before. When she finally stopped, she sashayed over to Liam, totally aware everybody was watching. With grand theatrics, she threw both her arms around his neck and kissed him square on the mouth, nearly knocking him over with her forward advance. All hands in the room clapped loudly, wolf whistles erupted, and a few eyes turned my way.

"I imagine you'd have something to say about this passionate display," said Deanna's father, who had materialized beside me.

"Not really," I said. "Do you?"

"You have to watch that one is all. She'll be the death of me one day, he said, cocking his head toward her.

"I hope not," I said.

"No harm done then?"

"No harm at all," I said.

It's funny how much bravado one comes up with when totally necessary. What was I supposed to say? *As a matter of fact, your daughter's behavior bothers me immensely, thank you for asking.* It seems with every new relationship, there are always a few landmines like Deanna's sister waiting to happen, and you never know when they're going to occur. Once they do, a lot of effort has to be put forth toward appearing nonchalant.

I watched as the stage area returned to normal. Deanna's sister found her way off of Liam, and into the arms of another unsuspecting bystander, and the night continued, deep in the throes of Irish traditional music well until one in the morning. Eventually the music just stopped, Liam put his accordion in the case, shook hands with his fellow musicians, and out the door we escaped for the journey back to Inverin.

A dense fog shrouded the night air as I turned to Liam and said, "You played well tonight."

"Did you enjoy yourself?" He glanced to his left.

"I did. It's amazing, whenever I go anywhere with you, I'm never really sure what it is I'm walking into— seems like it's always something."

"That's because people are always chatting you up," he flattered.

"That's the truth. I wish I had a dollar, I mean euro, for every time someone came up to me out of nowhere and asked if I came with you. Why is everyone so fascinated in whether or not I came with you?"

"Because I'm never seen with a woman," he answered quickly.

"Never?" I wanted more information.

"Not really, I actually don't have much experience in the ways of love," he said.

I took a minute with that. I was thinking, *how in the world could a guy who looks like Liam possibly be new to the ways of love, as he put it. Either the women around him were blind or stupid, and by the way, was this love?*

"I'm a little surprised at that," I finally said.

"Well, if you're thinking I'm a Don Juan, I'm not."

I was taken aback because he sounded defensive.

"No, I didn't think that, but I wouldn't hold it against you if you were. I just assumed women were throwing themselves all over you, that's all."

"Well, this is it, isn't it?" he said. "You could see how that would be a little off-putting."

"So, you've never been in a serious relationship?" I prodded.

"No, I never have. I've never been out with the same girl more than two or three times."

It hit me that I'd been out with Liam many more times than that. "Why only two or three times?"

"Women usually start expecting things of me after that," he said.

"I see." I started to get the picture. "You've just never felt the same."

"Not yet. What about you?"

"I have had a long relationship before," I said. "It's been a long time though."

"How long ago?"

"Years, four years or so. So long ago that things are kind of sketchy now."

"You know, I've thought about this before, and it really isn't any of my business what you did before I met you," he said.

"All right," I said, feeling a little cut off. "That's refreshing." *These kinds of conversations usually lead to a tangled web anyway,* I thought. *Still, a little background wouldn't be a bad thing, would it? Isn't that what people do? Isn't that how people get to know each other if they're really interested?* Maybe Liam didn't need to know anything about me, but I sure as hell wanted to know about him. Deciding there was nowhere else to go in the conversation, I left it alone.

We were well into the forlorn stretch of road that lies between Clifden and Inverin. The car's headlights sliced through the fog before us, casting a spotlight through a sense of timelessness in an area unmarked by time.

"It's lonesome out here," I said, staring out the window. "Spooky in a way."

"It is, yah. It's like this throughout most of Connemara if you go from one place to the next. You get used to it." The whir of the car's engine was pronounced in the dead silence as we drove onward.

Suddenly, as jolting as a scream, there flashed in the path of the headlights a seemingly disembodied face six feet up from the side of the road. Ghost white and deathly expressionless, the cadaverous face of a withered man shot into our view and just as quickly evaporated into dissipating vapor as the car sped past. I registered the apparition in a shocked, delayed reaction.

"What was that?" I looked at Liam, horrified. It was futile to point out there was nothing for at least thirty miles on either side of the road except bog land. Liam looked back at me without saying a word, he simply shot me a look with raised eyebrows.

I'd heard it recounted in Irish folklore that ghostly apparitions appeared in the strangest of places. Legend had it that the road closest to the coast was well traveled during famine times by battered, hungry, destitute families ejected from their homes. With immigration the only option, many families set out for the ports, but never made it to their destinations, so weary and broken were they from starvation. Tragically, some collapsed to their death on the road, and those who carried on had no means to transport the remains.

"I'm not sure what that was," Liam eventually said, "but out here there's a thin veil between this world and the next."

It was close to three in the morning when we pulled into my driveway under a pitch-black sky superimposed with a billion stars. "Will I come in, or will I go home and beg you to see me again tomorrow night?" Liam stopped the car.

"Definitely start begging me," I said. "You're wearing me out these days."

"All right, I'll wait," he said. "I've a session tomorrow night at Hughes, do you want to come with me?"

"Of course, what time do you start?"

"Not until nine, but I'll come for you at eight if that's to your liking," he said.

"Funny you should ask. That's exactly to my liking."

Chapter Eight

Pelting rain thrashed hard on the rooftop when the glass door rattled and slammed tersely shut on my front porch. It had been raining persistently all day with an inescapable howling wind that crept in and dampened every corner of my house. Liam stood on the doorstep looking windblown in the eight-o'clock hour of a Sunday night.

"Well, I'm here," he said, "a little worse for wear, but I'm here."

"I can't believe this weather," I said, opening the door.

"You learn to live with it. People are always running down the weather, but I think it's all in the attitude."

"Such is life," I said. "Should we get going?"

"We should, yah. We have to drive up the road to pick up my father first; he'll be playing tonight."

We scratched into the circular driveway of the modest one-level, whitewashed house, coming to a halt before the black, painted door. "I'll be right back," Liam said, jumping out.

I studied the surroundings through the car window. There was no yard to speak of, rather the house was positioned on the cusp of the bog that rambled on forever. Seconds later, Liam and his father emerged and approached on either side of the car. Noticing the large case in Liam's father's hands, I got out, offering him the front seat.

"You're all right there," Liam's father said, in an accent heavy with the hard, back of the throat tones of the Irish language. He was small and slightly built, with gray, steel-wool hair and blue-slate eyes. He looked to be in his late fifties, and I quickly assessed his face, trying to match its characteristics with Liam's. The strong, square jaw was there, as were the large, perfectly aligned teeth, but beyond that there were not many similarities. With impressive agility, he angled into the back seat, settling his instrument upon his lap, and commenting on the weather. "Ah, she's a fierce one, so she is," Liam's father said.

I noticed Liam was exceptionally formal and courteous to his father, coaxing a line of conversation from him as an adult would coax a response from a child. "And have you ever seen such a night, Da?" Liam asked encouragingly. His father paused, as if thinking it through. "Many a night indeed," his father returned. They went through so many rounds of this, it dawned on me his father did not have total command of the English language, and I knew they spoke it for my benefit.

Parking behind Hughes, we single-filed through a narrow hallway straight to the designated musicians' area, snug at the apex of two back walls. Burning turf glowed in the fireplace beside it, and I found a place in front of a window seat facing the inside of the room in clear view of the performance space. From that position, the crowd literally moved me wavelike until I was standing on the window seat, but at least I was out of harm's way. Loud chatter, flirting women, and posturing men rang in my ears, while pints of Guinness cluttered across tabletops like abstract art.

I watched a young man carrying a guitar approach the musicians corner, then a large, bear of a man sat down with a wooden marionette that kept time percussively on a plank balanced on his knee. They played with abandon and seemed oblivious to the racket around them, so intent were they in the consensus of their music. I stood watching Liam, who sat respectfully still, waiting to add the dancing personality that only the button accordion can bring. At one point, Liam played solo: a slow, ethereal, haunting tune that once ended, caused the other musicians to pause reflectively before they all launched again. It was another night in Hughes Pub; a night like many others with threatening rain outside, and the sweet, magic unification of music within.

When the music stopped, Liam gestured for me to come into the musicians' area where he introduced me to James—the man who held what I thought to be a marionette, but was actually an instrument called the clacker. Upon introducing me as an American, James stood up enthusiastically and lifted me off the ground in a big bear hug, then followed through by putting me down clumsily, which overturned a full pint of Guinness on my lap. Liam's father sat against the wall assessing with restrained owl eyes, as if waiting for my reaction, while Liam shot out of his chair, searching for something to mop up the beer. For an instant, I sat stunned, then I started laughing, which gave everyone else permission to do the same in a collective sigh of tension relieved.

"It's wetter in here than it is outside in the rain. I better take her safely home before anything else happens." Liam put an arm across my shoulders and shepherded me toward the door.

"You sure do have a way with the men," Liam shouted above the downpour. Slamming our car doors quickly, we backed out of Hughes' parking lot and made our way home, both of us clearing the exhaust from the inside of the windshield until we came to my driveway. Asking for my door keys, Liam jumped out of the car with the intention of grabbing the umbrella inside my porch. While I waited, a jolting knock sounded on the car window. I looked out, startled to see a man standing drenched from the rain, moving his lips. I rolled down the window and leaned forward as he continued his tirade in the Irish language. Feeling helpless, I hoped my eyes communicated I didn't speak his language. By the time Liam reappeared, I'd put two and two together.

"I think he wants you to move your car," I said.

An Irish dialogue ensued as the rain beat down against the top of the umbrella. Opening the car door, Liam handed it to me and encouraged me to go inside, but I was too fascinated listening to them talk. Watching Liam speak Irish fluently thrilled me because it added another dimension to his fabric, so I stayed on the wall in front of the house while they completed their business. Once Liam moved his car, I suddenly had an idea. "When was the last time you took a walk in the rain?"

"Practically every other day of my life, but I've never been looking for it."

"All right," I tried again. "When was the last time you took a walk in the rain with an American?"

"Never had the pleasure," he said. "Do you see the break in the clouds?" he pointed. It won't be raining much longer. We better go now if that's what you're after."

"Let's just walk down the road to the graveyard for a little while. My friend, Mick, says it's haunted."

"It is haunted," Liam said without hesitation.

"Says whom?"

"Well, I wouldn't know of it firsthand, but I have a cousin who swears by it. All our relatives are buried in the graveyard, so my cousin, Mary, goes often to tend to her mother's grave, like. She's told me she notices things."

"Notices things like what?" I wanted to know.

"Like the silence there for one. You never hear birds

singing, or notice any animals moving about, squirrels and that. There are many graves where grass won't grow as well, even though they've been there for decades. Mary says as hard as the wind can blow off the sea, what little grass there is remains undisturbed."

"So that means it's haunted?"

"That means it's unnatural, or perhaps supernatural." He emphasized the last word.

"It's not that I doubt you, but I've never heard of a supernatural graveyard."

"This one's different," he said, looking down the road.

"How's that?"

"Ancestors," he said. "In Connemara, we like to stay connected, you know. No need to be parted by a little thing like death. It may be that we as humans lack the faculties to perceive our ancestors—they're spirits now, they've changed form, so it's understandable we may not notice when they're around. My thinking is they know this, therefore they leave little clues. I think they'd like us to feel them every once in a while."

We stood beneath the umbrella before the low iron gate that partitioned the graveyard. "Your ancestors are in there?" I asked.

"All of them," he said. "I'll be there myself one day."

"Kind of a macabre thought," I said.

"Why? Don't you know where you're to be buried when your time comes?"

"Well, I wasn't planning on actually dying," I replied. "I was really planning on being air-lifted out of here like Elijah in his chariot."

"Right," said Liam. "Now if you've had enough of ghosts and sarcasm for one night, I'd like to get in out of this weather."

"Let's just take a quick look at the sea as long as we're here," I said.

Turning away from the gate, we continued up the road, then turned into the fields leading toward the sea. The wind had died down, turning the rain to mist by the time we arrived at the cliff overlooking the Atlantic, now tousling to an eddy from the abating rain.

"She's all but quiet now," Liam observed. "There now, can you see the birds coming back?" He pointed to a flock of black-headed gulls sailing seaward.

"Coming back from where?" I asked, straining my eyes in the moon's half-light.

"Inland. They fly inland before a rain. They always seek shelter before a storm," he said. "Birds instinctively know how to protect themselves from threat."

"I didn't know that," I said.

"Well, you wouldn't have to know these things living in a city as you have. Not much need to check the signs of nature now are there?"

"You're right about that. Anyway, I haven't always lived in a city, but just the same, I've never lived on an island. Signs from nature haven't exactly been a priority of mine, but I'll learn to amend my ways."

"Why don't you do that," he said.

The two sand-colored boulders at the tip of the ledge overlooking the sea gleamed spectrally in the moon's misty reflection. The drop to the sand below was only about eight feet, and I stood at the edge, looking down at the otherworldly moss-covered rocks that made a promenade into the sea. Turning around, I looked at Liam, who leaned against a boulder, watching me. Taking a few steps closer, I leaned into him and we stayed with our arms around each other, feeling the way we fit together, our cheeks lying gently side to side. I breathed in the scent of him; the feel of him, the novelty of him. My thoughts flashed, wondering if there'd ever be a day when I'd be used to him. He was so beautiful, so unlike anyone I'd ever known that I had yet to find my balance and was a little overwhelmed. I wondered if he could possibly feel the same, but realized there was no way of knowing.

We turned and started up the path that passed by the graveyard, falling into step with each other. "I'm sure you shouldn't be out this late," Liam said. "It's nearly one."

"You're right," I said. "Eight o'clock is going to come around early this morning. I can feel it already."

"If I don't take you home now, you won't let me come around again because I kept you up too late."

"Oh yah, I'll definitely punish you."

"How long do you usually stay at work?"

"A little before six, but it depends on what's happening. Sometimes it depends on what drama is revolving around Declan."

"He seems like that kind of guy," Liam said. *If he only knew the half of it,* I thought.

"Declan and Owen want me to hear Leigh McDonough play the Point in Dublin this Thursday night at ten o' clock. I'm trying to tell them I've seen her play many times before. It's not necessary for me to go all the way to Dublin to do it again. It'd put me back in Galway at four in the morning, which is asking a bit much," I said.

"Who is Owen?" Liam asked.

"That's a question I've been asking myself from the first time I met him," I laughed. "My understanding is this: he's the guy who's managing Leigh McDonough. The money to record her CD came from him, and he also gave the Centre money to keep operating. I don't know how much money he gave Declan, but it must be a lot. He thinks the Centre will help Leigh's career, and to put it plainly, Owen is the guy who is paying my salary."

"What's he get out of it?"

"I don't know, beyond seeing Leigh prosper," I said. "Owen was in Declan's life before I got here. He comes with the package as far as I can tell. Declan calls him his benefactor; that's all I know. We've been working on an application for financial backing from the Galway Arts Council since the day I started. I guess Owen's keeping things rolling until that happens. He thinks anything having to do with the Centre is in the interest of Leigh's career. Rumor has it Owen is in love with Leigh."

"I hope you don't go to Dublin this Thursday," said Liam. "I'd like to see you."

"I was going to ask you if you'd like to see a play at the Kings Head this Wednesday night," I said.

"What play?" he asked.

"Well, it's a one man show, really. There's an American actor named Brian Mallon whom I met through the Centre a while ago. He's a really nice guy from San Francisco—probably in his mid-forties or something. Just from talking to him you can tell he's talented; he kind of has that actor's edge, if you know what I mean. Shannon told me he's been a supporting actor in a few notable movies and that he comes to Ireland a few months out of every year to keep the creative flow going when he's not working in the US. Anyway, I'd like to see what he does," I said.

"So would I, so we'll go."

"Great," I said.

We reached the main road and crossed the street in front of my house. "Well, all right," said Liam. "Sleep well and I'll see you soon."

It occurred to me I could ask him exactly when he'd see me, but that would have disrupted the rhythm of the way Liam operated. In fine old Irish tradition, Liam just showed up when he was good and ready. I was used to that by now.

Chapter Nine

When the sun rose on Monday morning, I rose lazily with it. The light came warming through my windows at six thirty, and shortly thereafter I began to circle around the house in a long, relaxed preparation for meeting the morning bus into Galway. I knew I had plenty of time. It was going to be a fine day by the looks of things outside my window, and I stood for a while, watching the tide of the sea, wondering where the sheep that grazed in the field before it had come from overnight. I was halfway through my second cup of tea when suddenly and obtrusively, a knock clattered on the front door, calling me into unanticipated action.

I searched my memory, trying to recall if anybody had mentioned being on my doorstep at this hour. Insistently, the knock came again as I tightened the sash of my robe. Just as I considered the probability that this couldn't be good news, the knock repeated urgently. I pulled the door opened and was shocked to discover Declan and Owen standing in the porch.

"I'd like to chat to ya, Hailey," Owen fired in a businesslike tone, wearing a work shirt and jeans tucked into unlaced lumberjack boots, looking every bit the weathered, working-class man from Wales that he was.

"Is there anything wrong?" I said, not entertaining the possibility it could be otherwise.

"Declan tells me you're not going to Dublin to hear Leigh sing this week," he looked at me with blazing, challenging eyes. I looked over Owen's shoulder at Declan, who cowered sheepishly behind him, avoiding my gaze and looking down at the floor.

"That's right, I'm not. Is that what you're doing here at eight thirty in the morning?" I wanted to add the word "uninvited," but Owen was so hiked up, the implication probably would have gone right over his head.

"I just found this out last night," Owen fired.

"Did he just show up at your house this morning like this as well?" I said, looking straight at Declan. Declan continued looking at the floor with both hands tucked deeply in his pockets.

"I can't believe you're not going to hear her at The Point!" Owen accused. "This is her biggest show yet, a load of record people will be there, and you're on about not going."

"What difference does it make if I go or not, Owen?" I was missing the problem. "Why in the world would Leigh care if I'm there or not?"

"This is a big night for her! You helped produce her CD; you need to be there for her because you're part of this now."

"Then why is it you're standing on my porch instead of Leigh?"

"Because I look after her interests." Owen crossed his arms over his chest in body language that told me he wasn't open to much of anything I could say. It irritated me so much, I took a steadying breath. "Look, Owen, I don't want to be rude; I'm actually really trying to be tolerant here, but it seems like you're trying to muscle me around. I was happy to work with Leigh on the CD, but I work for the Centre, not exclusively for Leigh, and if you don't like the arrangement, then take it up with Declan." I kept looking over Owen's shoulder at Declan, wondering why he had, for the first time since I'd known him, decided to keep utterly mute.

The three of us stood in a long, pregnant pause. It

looked like Owen was thinking things through because his eyebrows were drawn tightly together and his forehead was in knots. Eventually, he relaxed and, as if continuing an entirely different conversation, he looked at me and said, "Would you be needing a lift into Galway, then?"

I guessed that concluded matters. *You really have to watch this guy,* I thought. My eyes found the clock. "All right," I said slowly. "Just wait a few minutes. I'll be right with you."

I left Owen and Declan standing on the porch and closed the front door behind me. I wasn't going to ask them in for a cup of tea, although that seemed to be the way everything in Ireland resolved itself. I was still too irritated with both of them for showing up out of nowhere and bringing their drama.

I got in the back of Owen's car, marveling at the way the two of them could so casually discuss the weather, as if there had never been another subject all morning. Dropping the subject in the interest of keeping the peace was one thing, dismissing it altogether was quite another. They kept up the inconsequential chitchat all the way into town, and by the time Owen dropped Declan and me off at the Centre, Shannon, Darren and Adrian were already there. I wasn't going to say anything to Declan with an audience around, so I waited for him to speak first. Eventually, he called a collective meeting in his most authoritative voice, and we all assembled upstairs in the loft.

"Does anybody have anything to say?" He rolled up his shirtsleeves and looked furtively at me. We all looked back at Declan and waited. "Right, then." He cleared his throat. He picked up his notepad and categorically went down a short list of projects we had in play. Shannon and I had been working on the press kit of an exceptional singer/songwriter from County Mayo named Jason Kearney. We'd written a cover page and organized his press releases by date so we could send it around to the Irish record labels along with his three-song demo. Declan looked at the finished pamphlet, nodded importantly, and suggested we offer the same for a handful of other musicians around town.

"We need to be charging more for this service because we're losing money," Shannon reported.

"So, we'll move it to thirty euros to do the entire thing," Declan said. "I think we should have bands come in downstairs and rehearse here if they want to. There's not another space in Galway where bands can rehearse, and I've been thinking we can charge ten euros an hour for the room once we clear it out a little. We'll have to advertise, but it'll probably be word of mouth that brings them in."

"We're going to have to soundproof the room downstairs first," Darren said, "and what about a drum kit? We're going to have to have one in there permanently; bands don't drag around their drum kit, only guitars and the like."

"What do you think Bernard's going to say about that?" I asked.

"If we soundproof the room, he won't hear a thing from his house," Declan pointed out.

"We're going to have to clear it with him first since he owns the forge," Darren added.

"I'll chat to Bernard," said Declan. "Does anybody else have anything to say?" He looked straight at me. We all kept silent, deferring to each other. "Right," said Declan, standing up and ending the meeting. "Hailey, can I chat to you for a second?"

"Sure," I said. I followed Declan into the courtyard.

"Let's walk a while," he said, leading the way.

I kept thinking Declan sure had changed his demeanor since earlier that morning. I walked beside him patiently, wondering what he was going to do next. The bounce in his walk practically defied gravity; he was built so compactly and was so light on his feet that the sway of his rhythm caused the ponytail on the back of his head to swing side to side. I kept thinking there was something so perfectly analogous of Declan's capricious attitude in the movement.

I followed Declan to the Eglington Canal, where he finally sat down and patted the grass beside him. I sat down, waiting. I wasn't going to be the first to speak. I was pretty sure Declan wanted me to yell at him, or at least give him something to defend against, so I did the exact opposite. *Better to let him twist in the wind a while*, I thought. *Serves him right.*

"All right, say something," Declan erupted.

"About what, this morning?" I feigned disinterest.

"Yah, about this morning," he said quickly, his voice unable to hide his impatience.

I took a deep breath. "All right, you two were totally out of line. I'm annoyed with you for standing there mutely while Owen was completely off his rocker. What's wrong with the guy? Do you think I'm working for Leigh McDonough, or are we all working for the Centre?"

"We work for the Centre, of course," Declan retorted.

"Then what were you doing acting like Owen's wingman? I'm curious: did he just show up at your house to get you this morning? Did you know he was coming?"

"No, I didn't know he was coming, but when he did, I just got in the car because he seemed so wound up. I don't want to mess with a guy like Owen; I'm not sure of his background, if you take my meaning. "

"I don't take your meaning," I said.

"Owen's got Irish connections," he said.

"So what?

"Northern Irish connections."

"All right, so whatever. Why didn't you straighten him out? All you had to do was tell him what we just settled: that I work for the Centre. You could've saved both of you the trouble of driving all the way out to Inverin," I said.

"I had no idea why you didn't want to go to Leigh's show. I didn't know what to tell him."

"Why does it even matter? I swear, neither one of you makes sense. Couldn't you have figured out that Owen was just throwing his weight around? It was like having a thug show up at your door threatening you," I said. "It's a hell of a way to get up in the morning. Remind me to do it to you some day."

"I'm sorry, Hailey," he said, but he still had a disarming twinkle in his eye, as if he were really amused. Declan was always at his best whenever drama was happening.

"Well, if you're trying to permanently irritate me, just keep it up." Neither of us said anything for a minute. I figured we were both looking for a way to end the matter because there was nowhere else to go.

"I'm going to marry you one day, you know," Declan said, standing up as if that concluded things.

"I bet you say that to all the girls," I said, brushing the grass from my pants.

We headed back to the Centre, and when we reached the driveway, Declan threw his arm across my shoulder, pulling me off balance. "I'm still going to marry you," he said with that boyish look in his eyes.

"Declan, get your arm off of me," I swatted him away. But it was still kind of funny.

It took me a while to figure out, but Declan was definitely one of those guys who only know one way to relate to a woman. Sooner or later, he'd resort to turning on the charm if he felt he wasn't making progress otherwise. I didn't hold this against him; rather, I saw it as an obstacle I had to repeatedly navigate. It presented itself every time we had to talk seriously about anything. It seemed it was Declan's tactic for the purpose of deflection, and he would employ it each time he felt he was losing ground.

Shannon once pointed out that I should take it easy on Declan. "He's twenty-five, but he's a young twenty-five," Shannon had said, and I knew just what she meant. Declan had so much energy and such inflated good intentions that he sometimes got in over his head with people. He wanted to be in charge, and we all encouraged his leadership, it was just that if anyone presented him with an idea, he spent a lot of time weighing it out, as if he were doing so against the measuring stick of his profound wisdom and vast experience.

He liked to make us wait for him to think things through, and we were in the habit of playing the game and waiting, but we only waited to ascertain whether there needed to be more convincing from our part. Over time, the dynamic became a trial, but in the early days of the Galway Music Centre, Declan's personality, ambition and showmanship was the hub of the wheel the rest of us revolved around.

* * *

In the courtyard, Darren and Adrian were sunning themselves on the ledge outside the stained glass workshop, which lay next door to the Centre. Darren lay on his back with a cigarette dangling between two fingers of his outreached hand. His bleached-blond hair fanned out beneath him, and his long-sleeved shirt was unbuttoned all the way down, laying opened on either side of him. He rose when he spied Declan and me walking up the driveway.

"I talked to Bernard." Darren sat up. "He says it's fine for us to start a rehearsal business here, but we're definitely going to have to soundproof the walls. Ian next door will help us do it, and Bernard says he went to school with a guy who owns a music store up the road; we should call out to him about the drums."

"That's incredibly nice of Bernard," I said. "Really, we'd be doing something structurally permanent to the forge, and he's all right with it. It's unreal."

"He thinks we may have something here, a good money-making scheme. Bernard said he'd ask your man to donate the drums if we wanted," Adrian added.

"Now Bernard's working for us? This is great!" I enthused.

"I'll go into town and tell the *Advertiser* we're offering a new service and either make an announcement, or place an ad," Adrian continued.

"Wait until we have another meeting before you do that, Adrian," Declan cut him off. "We'll have to figure out a few things and get the room built first."

A blush colored Adrian's face as he turned away from Declan. "Two guys called in for you while you were gone." It took me a second to realize Adrian was talking to me.

"Did you get any names?" I looked at Adrian.

"Mick from Inverin."

"Are they coming back?"

"I think so," he said.

As it turned out, Mick never came back to the Centre that day, but the next afternoon, I ran into him by chance. He was standing at the Centra's gas pump in Inverin, across the street from where I lived, and I noticed him the second I dismounted the bus from Galway. His wavy hair obscured his face while he pumped gas into his van.

"I'm sorry I missed you yesterday," I said, walking over to him.

"I'm sorry meself, and my friend as well," Mick said.

"Who was that?"

"One of the lads from Clonmel I've known for ages. He was just here overnight. I thought I'd bring him round since we were in Galway for the day."

"So, he's gone now?"

"Oh yah, and it's just as well, since I'm leaving me wife just now," he said. "I'm leaving and not keen to go back. Told her straight away, so I did."

I paused for a split second thinking I probably shouldn't pursue this, but there was no pretending I hadn't heard what he'd said. Sooner or later I was going to have to comment.

"Where are you going?" I asked.

"I'm just going, is all. Don't ever get married!" He walked around from the other side of the van, coming closer to me.

"But you're not married," I reminded him.

"Well, you should try telling her that; she thinks she owns me, that one does," he huffed.

I didn't want to get further involved in whatever it was that was happening between Mick and Gabrielle—I didn't want to know the details. I didn't want to be privy to information coming from his side of things because it would have put me more firmly in his camp at the exclusion of Gabrielle's, and I wanted to remain impartial. I was too new to both of them, and I thought I should remain safely ensconced in neutrality. We stood looking at each other for a second longer.

"Sometimes a little distance isn't a bad thing," I finally said. "Give it a chance to cool down a bit."

Mick circled back around and closed his gas tank. He'd obviously finished what he came to the Centra to do. "I guess I'll see you later." I started backing away.

"Right," he said, in a flurry of frenetic energy that radiated in every exaggerated, steam-blowing gesture he made from slamming the door of the gas tank to slamming the car door with a mean clap.

I turned and headed up the road toward my house thinking it sounds like a lover's quarrel to me, yet in this moment of heated separation, to them it was probably the end of the world. In the course of time, once Mick calmed down to a semblance of a manageable perspective, he'd have to go home. I pondered how that would be when he did: that seminal instance of reentry, the shame-faced readdress of words unleashed from a defensive ego which thought it was right and the other was wrong.

They'd test the waters in awkward, unhealed silences, licking their own wounds and wondering if they'd gone too far in the other's eyes while they waited for the balance in the rhythm of their love to return as if nothing had ever happened. I didn't envy either of them their current plight, and my chest tightened as I remembered love can have such a terrible downside. I put my key in the door to the living room, thinking it's a wonder people tie up with each other for any sustainable length of time in the first place. Once they do, the pity is so many people mishandle it.

Chapter Ten

Brian Mallon's one-man show at the Kings Head was entitled, "A Hoor for the Poetry." It was actually a recitation of twelve of his favorite Irish poems embellished with one prop: a Connemara tweed cap woven in threads of earth-toned beige, which he stashed in his back pocket until the moment of need. He performed in the same room we'd used for the showcase, but the stage had been moved to the opposite wall, and a bar was arranged to the left of five eighteen-foot wooden tables lined in a row before the stage. Taking center seats in the second row, Liam and I flipped through our programs.

It was astounding to watch Brian Mallon as he went from one character to another, lending the perfect pitch to each poem. He deftly changed accents, employing a Scottish burr, a Yank from the States, and a spot-on Connemara accent, which came to life as he pulled out the hat and set it half-mast above his eyes, the way they wear such a cap in the Aran Islands. His posture changed, his face changed, his demeanor changed with eyes that found different levels of intensity as the soul of the poems moved through him in a delivery so naturally authentic they each seemed an intimate monologue. Liam and I were riveted, and spoke not a word to each other during the entirety of the show, with the exception of the beginning of William Butler Yeats' poem, "Never Give All the Heart."

"I know this one!" Liam tapped me on the shoulder and smiled with unmistakable pride at the words of his countryman as Brian Mallon placed a hand to his heart and stood tall.

> "Never give all the heart, for love
> Will hardly seem worth thinking of
> To passionate women if it seem
> Certain, and they never dream
> That it fades out from kiss to kiss;
> For everything that's lovely is
> But a brief, dreamy, kind delight.
> O never give the heart outright,
> For they, for all smooth lips can say,
> Have given their hearts up to the play.
> And who could play it well enough
> If deaf and dumb and blind with love?
> He that made this knows all the cost,
> For he gave all his heart and lost."

Brian Mallon looked straight into the audience with spell-casting vehemence so that the words of the poem took on a level of sincerity that turned it into a conversational monologue. Liam drew in his breath at the end of the poem, folded his hands in front of him and looked over at me, nodding his approval.

As witnessing a great performance often does, at the end of the show, I felt as though I'd been through an enlivening, visceral experience. We went to the bar, joining the queue where Brian was standing, shaking hands and signing programs, receiving us all with touching humility and grace. In that moment, I was proud to have Liam meet an American the likes of Brian because I knew Liam thought of Americans much in the way many in Ireland do: we're culturally bereft, too direct, and unfamiliar with the concept of subtlety, so the way I saw it, Brian Mallon put a good name on America.

In the summer months, the sun shines eighteen hours a day in Ireland, not setting until well after ten thirty at night. In early October, there's a sense of change in the air as Ireland inches out of daylight savings time at the end of the month. It was still light as we drove the coast road from Galway to Spiddal in the eight o'clock hour of early October, but like a homing pigeon observing the clock not the sun, Liam pulled off the main road and parked in the lot behind Hughes.

I waited while Liam went to the bar and chatted with Bridgid, the well-loved matriarch of Hughes Pub. I saw her lean around Liam's shoulder for a clear view of me, but I couldn't hear what they were saying. I was getting used to being on display when I was with him, and was at the point where it didn't faze me anymore. Liam came ambling over with a glass in each hand. I took the half-pint and scooted my chair back so he could settle in beside me.

"Right, here we are now at my second home," he said in all seriousness.

I smiled, but what I was thinking was having a pub as a second home wouldn't be a good sign if we were in any other country. I couldn't help but notice Liam seemed pensive. His wasn't saying anything and his gaze was focused somewhere on the floor.

"What are you thinking?" I eventually asked.

"Well, I'm thinking about the show we just saw," he said, his eyes now focused on me.

"Brian Mallon's something else, isn't he?" I said.

"He is, yah, but specifically, I was thinking about the Yeats poem." I waited for him to continue, but he didn't elaborate.

I'm going to have to ask him what he's thinking again, I thought. "What about it?" I asked, thinking, *I'm pulling teeth here.*

"What do you think about not giving all of the heart?" he said quickly.

"As a principle?"

"Yah," he said.

I didn't know if I should be on guard or open-minded. I'd watched Liam's body language enough to know he was pondering his own stance on the subject. I decided I had nothing to lose by telling him what I thought.

"I think it's a limited way to go about life," I said. "Anyway, that's not at all what I think about giving the heart. Sometimes you just have to take a dare, take a risk, so to speak, without any expectations. It's the goal-orientated attitude that trips us up sometimes, you know?"

"What do you mean?" he said.

"Well, it's like the path is more important than the goal, and you can't hold yourself back because you're afraid of the goal, or because you don't know exactly what the goal is going to look like. You'd be missing the experience if you did."

Liam looked painfully confused.

"I think I agree," he said, but the tilt of his head didn't convince me.

I had a feeling Liam didn't know if he agreed or not, his tone of voice seemed too uncertain. Maybe he'd think about it later and arrive at another conclusion. He seemed so young to me in that moment. He was shedding light on his inexperience, but he had told me before he was inexperienced in the ways of love. For some reason, I couldn't bring myself to completely buy it. No matter how many times Liam told me, I could not fathom a guy like him being so novice when it came to women. I still doubted he hadn't been around the block more than he claimed. It just seemed unusual.

"Have you ever been rejected?" he suddenly asked.

Where in the world is this conversation going? I thought.

"Not really," I said, even though that wasn't entirely true. I could have been specific, but I didn't trust his line of questioning.

"How would you feel if you were to be rejected?" he continued.

Not good, I thought. *Is he trying to tell me something?*

"I don't know," I said. "I'd like to think I'd be all right. I'd try to be philosophical."

It's time to turn the tables on him, I thought. "What about you?" I said.

He looked at my half-finished pint and said, "You want another one?" In a flash, he was up and walking toward the bar.

Nice deflective move, I thought.

The next day at the Centre, I told Shannon about the conversation. "The boy is in pain," she concluded summarily.

"What am I, part of his learning curve?"

Shannon didn't hesitate. "Probably so."

I would have loved further insight from Shannon, but there wasn't exactly anything else she could have said. Still, I was disturbed by something I couldn't identify, and that's the worst kind of disturbance. I've never liked ambiguous situations. I jump to too many conclusions.

"When are you going to see him again?" Shannon asked.

"I'm not sure. He'll be going out of town in a few days; I do know that. He and a few musicians are getting on a boat and sailing from port to port where they'll play in a handful of pubs. He said they do that every year. He asked if I wanted to meet the boat at the Spiddal Pier when it comes in this Sunday."

"Do you want us to come out and go with you?" she offered.

"I don't know. Let me think about it. Let me see what's going to happen between now and then. I feel kind of off-center right now. You know what? He's never even asked me how old I am. We've never gotten around to any normal line of questioning."

"And he doesn't care about your past either," she said flatly.

"Is this weird?" I asked. "I could be forty for all he knows. I could be forty with three children in America," I said. "I could be forty with three children in America that I used to tolerate before I had a nervous breakdown and ax-murdered all of them."

"And now you're on the run in another country," she said.

"Exactly! Lord, I sure know how to pick 'em."

"Don't say that yet."

"All right. You're right," I resigned.

Deanna Rader came floating into the Centre as Shannon and I sat talking. She had an unwieldy guitar case in her hand that was almost bigger than she.

"Is Declan around?" She set the case down.

"Declan's not here," I told her. "He was earlier. He went up the road to buy some girl a dozen roses."

"Declan's on the hunt," Shannon said, and we all laughed.

"Declan's been on the hunt since the day I met him." Deanna pulled up a chair and sat down.

"He tried to bribe Hailey and me into doing the deed

for him," Shannon told Deanna.

"Did you tell him to do his own romancing, then?" Deanna looked at me.

"I told him I wasn't going to be his secretary, but I don't think he got the joke."

"Well, I'll have a cup of tea then." Deanna got up and pressed the top of the electric kettle.

"We're out of milk," Shannon said.

"Can't have that. I'll call out to the shop on Mill Street and be right back." Deanna accepted the money Shannon handed her and walked out the door.

When Deanna returned, the three of us drank cup after cup of tea and talked companionably about trivialities until Shannon looked at her watch, saying, "It's half five, let's close for the day. I'm going home to wait for Darren."

As I turned out the lights and locked the Centre's flimsy wood door, Deanna asked if I wanted to go into town.

"To where?" I asked.

"Up to Eyre Square for a bit," she said. "I'll drive you out to Inverin later on if you'd like."

We rounded the gray concrete sidewalk to Deanna's two-story, rented house on Henry Street to drop off her guitar before setting out for Eyre Square. Her house was simple inside, with stucco walls faded to a lusterless cream color and cold, stone floors covered with well-trodden rugs. The ceilings were high and a large fireplace graced the living room where a blue-painted staircase lifted from the floor to the warped floor above where two bedrooms lay. An open dining room lay in the back of the first floor, and the kitchen jutting off it looked like it had once been a garage. It was typical of the houses in Galway City's interior, and was full of earthy, utilitarian character with gritty, old-world charm.

It took us forty-five minutes to walk through town because six people stopped us on our way to Eyre Square. That's usually the case in Galway City; you can't just walk down the street from source to destination without stopping to talk to a handful of people because everybody's hanging around like they've got all the time in the world. It's a similar mentality to that found in Inverin. It's unthinkable just to send a wave and unpardonable not to stop because that would be an antisocial crime against Irish society.

Deanna lowered her voice to a confidential tone as we progressed up Shop Street. "Did you know Mary O'Toole's been in love with Liam Hennessey for ages?"

"Who's Mary O'Toole?" I asked.

"She's the sister of Sean O'Toole, who plays with Liam sometimes. Of course, Liam won't give her the time of day but oh, how she moons over him! She's absolutely desperate. He's not an easy one, our Liam."

"Have you ever known him to be with a girl?" I asked.

"Never the one," she said. "I don't see Liam that often, but when I do, he's always on his own."

"I guess he's just a loner," I said. "I don't know, seems like a riddle to me. I wonder what he's doing coming around to me all the time."

"He fancies you, I don't know what else it could be. Wait, I've a brilliant idea: you should meet Harriet," she said, swatting me on the arm as if the idea just hit her.

"Who's Harriet?"

"She's a Tarot card reader. She's mighty good at it, too."

"Has she read cards for you?"

"Many times, and she's always spot-on. Harriet's one

of the wise ones; she's from the old guard, definitely fey. Most Celts are one way or another. You're one of us, anyone could tell from the look of ya, so you probably are as well but nobody can see their own stuff as well as someone like Harriet. It'd just be a good idea to have her take a look at you. "

"What kind of cards does she read?"

"She has the Crowley deck, the one with the great pictures on it. The cards are huge," she said. I'll take you to meet her any time you want."

"All right, I'll think about it," I said. *And I would, if things came to that. I'd have to ponder that for a while. Ireland has such a reputation for the mystical. If this woman can indeed read cards she's no doubt really good at it, and that would be something I might as well experience as long as I'm here,* I thought.

I stayed with Deanna until eleven o'clock that night. Most of the time we spent in Taylor's Pub talking to Declan who, it turned out, was on the hunt for the barkeeper there whose name was Helen. She was a shy, fragile-looking blonde who couldn't look at Declan without shaking. She seemed absolutely overwhelmed by Declan's attentions, which were evident from the vase of red roses sitting before the mirror of the bar. Declan and Deanna joined a session going on in the backroom, where Declan played guitar and Deanna stood in the middle of the semicircle singing in her deep-throated voice. As far as attention goes, Deanna drew the attention of most of the patrons of Taylor's that night, and Declan could not draw the attention of Helen enough, though he spent the entire night trying.

I closed the car door behind me and leaned in to Deanna. "Thanks for driving me all the way out here. I really appreciate it."

"You'd do the same for me," she said with a wave.

I turned on the porch light and saw a small piece of white paper on the porch table. It was a record of a withdrawal from the Bank of Ireland that had a hand-written account number on it and forty pounds specified in the withdrawal box just above the name Liam Hennessey. Curious, I turned it over to the other side and realized it had been used as a scrap of notepaper.

"Dear Hailey,

Sorry to have missed you.

We should have made arrangements, but then last night's parting was inexplicably restrained. Anyhow, I was hoping to spend tomorrow night with you if you're agreeable to that.

Please ring me tomorrow:

593814.

Love and kisses,

Liam."

I couldn't believe it. I was thinking how poetically Liam writes. I was also thinking the reason things were "inexplicably restrained" was because Liam had been talking about rejection and acting cagey. Also, it seemed clear to me there was something about the predicament Liam found himself in that made him uncomfortable. I'd noticed after each night of parting, it was as if the next time I saw him, familiar terrain had to be retread all over again before he'd relax. Then I started thinking I was going to be uncomfortable "ringing Liam" because with my luck, his mother would answer and I'd feel like some brazen girl from America trying to nab her child. I walked inside and decided to worry about it the next day.

I must have thought about it a dozen times, but never could settle upon a good time to call Liam's house. The exaggerated image I conjured placed him in the kitchen protectively flanked by both his parents as the telephone rang. I pictured his father answering the phone, speaking in Irish then switching to English at the intrusive sound of my voice asking for his son. He would have to explain my call to Liam's mother, who would slightly frown and remain purposefully still in order to overhear Liam's end of the conversation.

I was pretty sure she thought she should guard him from the danger of an American. Further, if the Hennesseys attitude toward the phone was like everybody else's I'd observed in rural Ireland, then the phone being used in any capacity was a very big deal. Phones are not used recreationally in rural Ireland; they always mean big business, and my phone call to Liam would be perceived as a tactless American wanting something from Liam. I doubted if he'd volunteer to his parents that he'd asked me in writing to call him.

No doubt, it would appear I was audaciously tracking him down, going against the laws of nature to ask him for a date. I had it all worked up in my mind, and felt damned if I did, and damned if I didn't call. I spent the day at the music center turning it over to the point of paralysis. Eventually, I conceded if I waited until I got to Inverin, then at least nobody would be around to overhear me call; at least I wouldn't be handing Declan something in which to sink his teeth. I finally settled upon going home, collecting my calling card for the phone booth at the Centra, and calling Liam. It turned out I didn't have to, for when I walked into my porch, Liam was casually sitting there looking right at home.

"I was just going to call you," I spilled out, noticing Liam had a rather eyebrows raised, quizzical look on his face.

"I was just up the road, so I thought I'd call in to see if you were home." He leaned back casually, crossing his legs.

"Up the road doing what?"

"Playing handball at the school there," he said, nodding in the direction of the school up the road behind my house.

I turned and looked through the glass door. I'd never once seen any activity anywhere around the school. I didn't think the school was even open.

"You play handball?" I asked without stopping to think. I just couldn't picture it.

"Oh yah, we should play sometime," Liam said.

"All right," I said, hoping that would never happen.

"I was also thinking, just last night as a matter of fact, I'd like to take you to Coole Park in Gort sometime. I'd like you to see where Yeats spent a lot of his time."

"All right," I said.

So, he's making plans, I thought.

After a pregnant pause wherein Liam seemed to be studying me, he finally said, "I called out to see you last night."

"I know, I got your note."

Liam hesitated while I stood there wondering if I was supposed to volunteer my whereabouts the night before. He kept looking at me intently, so I returned his gaze and waited.

"Can I get you anything?" I asked him.

"Were you out late?" he resumed, a feigned casualness to his voice.

"Not very late, maybe eleven thirty or so."

I waited for the next question. *Surely, he's leading up to something,"* I thought. "Are you sure I can't get you anything? A cup of tea, maybe?"

"No, thank you. Actually, I was thinking I'd like to collect you in a few hours, if you're not doing anything tonight," he said, emphasizing the words "doing anything."

"I'm not doing anything tonight," I said, getting the picture.

Liam's fidgeting discomfort was starting to amuse me. I was thinking of an acting class I took in college wherein the teacher encouraged us to pay attention not to what the characters said, but to the words left unsaid. "This is called the characters' subtext, and therein lays the motivation of each character," the teacher had said. Liam's subtext flattered me in some strange way; I could read it all over his face. I added everything together quickly: he had come to see me last night, and I had not been home.

There was no appropriate way for him to ask me where I'd been, but he definitely wanted to know. He was taking great pains to appear nonchalant, but I was aware of his discomfort and it charged the air between us. I started thinking I had a couple of choices: I could address his unspoken questions voluntarily and reveal last night's detailed itinerary, or I could leave him guessing. I decided leaving him guessing was infinitely the better way to go.

"My father is playing at the Cruiscan at ten. I'll go get cleaned up and come back here later," he said, standing up.

"What time?" I asked.

"Nine thirty or so."

"Okay," I agreed, holding the door open.

I looked at the clock and knew I had plenty of time to

go out for a walk, which always cleared my head, so I put on my tennis shoes and set out for the bog thinking that's enough wondering about what's going on with Liam for now. I walked toward the Centra, turned left, and travelled the road into the heart of the bog. I was now familiar with every flowing angle of the dirt and gravel road, and I loved the sense of time suspension it always seemed to give me. I did my best thinking on these walks; for one, all too brief moment, I could quiet the chattering voice in my head and just look around in the moment as I beat out in steps what seemed like a walking meditation. With the contrast of the bog before me and the sea at my back, each time I walked the area, I felt a little more anchored to the spirit of Connemara and it soothed me in that way a sense of belonging often does.

At ten o'clock, Liam and I stood out on the coast road in Spiddal, in front of the Cruiscan Lan. The daylight had fallen to a waning half-light, and the road that runs through Spiddal is only dimly lighted in erratic places, leaving pockets of dark gray in contrast. Silent as a specter, Liam's father materialized from around the corner carrying his melodeon case, flanked by two older women. Liam stepped forward gallantly, kissing both women in turn on either side of her face while neither made a secret of appraising me.

"Liam, where do you come up with these blondes?" one of them asked, removing herself from Liam's embrace.

Although I knew it was supposed to be some sort of compliment, I still wondered if the implication was that Liam appeared with blondes on a regular basis.

"This is Hailey from America," Liam introduced.

"I'm Mrs. Fahey and this is my sister, Mrs. Wallace,"

she beamed at me.

"It's nice to meet you both," I said. I looked over at Liam's father, who stood silently studying me. He seemed to do a lot of that when I was around.

"We've known Liam here since he was a wee lad," Mrs. Fahey continued. "If it's stories you're after, come to us!"

"Is that right?" I asked for lack of anything better to say. I'd noticed that rhetorical questions go a long way in Ireland.

"'Tis," she responded. "We've watched this one grow, so we have."

Mrs. Fahey was the likable sort. She wore a khaki colored wraparound skirt with a white cotton cardigan and sensible shoes. Her sister was similarly dressed, and they both had hair cut in the same style, bleached the exact same color of blonde. When one of them spoke, the other stood smiling, as if they were both part of the same dialogue.

"Will the two of youse be coming in, then?" Mrs. Wallace turned to Liam.

"Right behind you," he said, taking my hand.

There was enough activity inside the Cruiscan to lose sight of Liam's father until the music began. An area in the back spontaneously formed a semicircle before the seated musicians and the second they started to play, the room's chatter subsided. On the dance floor, couples of all ages two-stepped, sidestepped, and twirled in deliberate steps that landed heavily in unison with the music. I'd never seen this kind of dancing before, so I focused on one couple until I deciphered their repeated steps.

"Now I get what they're doing," I said to Liam.

He raised his eyebrows in answer. "I haven't a clue

what they're doing at all," he said.

"Watch these two over here," I said, pointing. "One two, one two, one two, and turn. It's like the waltz." Liam nodded.

We watched the people in the crowd for a couple of hours. It was enough just to be in the room, for the crowd became its own sphere of panoramic entertainment. Within the mayhem of dancers and drinkers, a general atmosphere thrived of joy in motion. Its mood was contagious, its attitude inclusive, and I couldn't help being tossed by its festive tide. Eventually saturated, we walked out to the street, physically affected from the energy in the room.

"Where would you like to go next, Hughes?" Liam stopped for a second.

"I can't get involved in another scene like that," I said. "I can only do one Spiddal pub a night; then I have to draw the line."

"All right, home, is it?"

"Way too early for that."

"Shall we walk, then?"

"Great idea."

"Let's walk up the road to the Spiddal Pier," Liam said.

"You ever notice how everything around here is just up the road? It doesn't matter what you're talking about, or how far the distance; it'll still be just up the road."

Liam gave me a crooked smile. "Well, actually, sometimes it's just down the road."

From my point of view, there was something about Liam that was entirely capable of standing in witness of his own Irishness, as if he were an outsider recognizing his own cultural absurdity. Because he was able to stand apart from it, he never took my questions or observations personally; rather, he donned a surprising self-deprecation, but it was tinged with national pride.

We turned right at the church, walked the gravel road to the pier, and then climbed the ledge until we came to its edge above the sea.

"This is where we'll dock next weekend," Liam reminded me.

I was about to say something, but suddenly a voice called out from the other side of the wall.

"Is that you there?" the voice rang. I was startled—I didn't know there was another ledge jutting out from the other side of the wall. Liam hoisted himself to the top, leaned over, and looked down.

"Whatever in the world are you doing there?" I heard him say. A head popped up from the other side of the wall. It was Patrick.

"We were just on about doing a little night fishing," he said, in a voice coy as a gentle wind.

Liam lowered himself, and around from the walls' edge walked Patrick and a girl I'd never seen before.

"Hiya, Hailey." Patrick nodded toward me.

"Nice night," I returned, looking from Patrick to the girl at his side.

"This is Evie." Patrick threw a muscular arm around her.

"Nice to meet you, Evie," I said, smiling.

Even though we were on the sheltered side of the wall, the chilled, damp air whipped around us. Evie stood with her hands buried into her blue-jean jacket. She couldn't bring herself to meet my gaze.

"So, you were at the Cruiscan, you were," Patrick stated.

"We were, yah," Liam confirmed. The two friends looked at each other levelly. I got the feeling something was being left unsaid.

"Nice crowd, was it?" Patrick continued.

"All the usual," Liam reported. Patrick kept staring at Liam.

"Anyone know you're here?" He shifted his weight.

"Not a living soul," Liam returned.

"Well then, there it is," Patrick concluded with a note of satisfaction. "Will you join us for a can?"

Seemingly out of thin air, Patrick produced two cans of Guinness, and we all sat down, leaning back against the wall of the Spiddal Pier.

"I imagine you'll be taking off this Wednesday, when is it, noon?" Patrick looked at Liam.

"I still wish you'd change your mind and come with us," Liam said.

"Not a snowball's chance in hell. I won't be going anywhere Steve is going and there's an end to it." Patrick sounded final.

"There's an end to it? What will it be next; you'll be canceling all your gigs about town?"

"I'll do what needs to be done."

"And your brother, Sean?" Liam asked. "Are you on about him as well, or is it just Steve?"

"Well, Sean's the one who hit me in the face now, isn't he? Seems his loyalties lay with Steve."

I watched the two as if I were watching a tennis match. I had to ask, "Where did this happen?"

"At the Kings Head in front of God and everybody," answered Patrick.

"Over what?" I asked, thinking I'm already in it now. I half expected Patrick not to answer.

"Over Steve thinking he's better than Springsteen with all his original songs, and telling the band what we will, and will not be playing. I didn't come to Connemara for this shite. I'm not looking to be a part of his back-up band," Patrick said.

"Can't you do both without it coming to fists?" Liam suggested.

"Not with that one, you can't," Patrick spat. "Give him an inch and he takes over altogether. On top of that, Steve's proclaimed I'm not that hot of a fiddler, that he's looking for a bass player, and by the way, why don't I just switch to the bass seeing as how it suits the needs of himself; then he can save us all future embarrassment from my amateur fiddling," Patrick said, in a monologue like rapid gunfire.

It was all starting to come together for me. Looking at Patrick against the background of the night, I thought he's one of those guys who can wear anger in such a way that it enhances the look of him.

"I don't want to put you in the middle of this, Liam," Patrick said, toning down his anger.

"Not at all," Liam dismissed.

"Look, if you're still planning on touring New Zealand with them, then be my guest, and no harm done, fair play to ya."

"Fair enough," said Liam. "I'll think about it."

Patrick leaned forward, looking at me. "Hailey was just starting to like the band," he said.

"This is nothing new to me," I said. "I mean, there's nothing surprising when you're talking about a group of creative musicians. Temperaments are going to clash sooner or later. I don't mean to generalize or sound derogatory, it's just kind of the way it is."

"Ah yes," said Liam. "We're all temperamental children, the lot of us."

"From your mouth to God's ear," added Patrick.

"Oh, good, at least you can see the humor," I said.

"Anyway, it's not like you're going to quit playing or anything, right?"

"Not at all, I'll just find something else, plain and simple," he said, "Galway's crawling with musicians."

Patrick had a point: musicians were all over Galway. It seemed everyone I'd met in town played an instrument, and most of the musicians knew each other. I thought of Mick Folan. "I know a guy you should meet: his name is Mick Folan, he lives in the bog behind me. He's originally from Clonmel. He writes his own songs, and plays great guitar; seriously, he's really good. He knows all the trad tunes; you two should meet."

"Any friend of yours," Patrick trailed off.

Evie never said a word the entire time, yet she broke up the scene by standing up tentatively, hands still in her pockets, eyes cast to the ground as if signaling she was ready to leave. As Liam and I walked back down the road, I asked if Patrick had been asking whether we'd seen Steve and Sean in the Cruiscan.

"That's not what he was asking," Liam answered. "He wanted to know if we'd seen Malia."

"Who's Malia?" I asked.

"Patrick's girlfriend."

"Okay." I didn't skip a beat. "Was she there?"

"Oh, she was there, all right. She was standing across the room with a pack of girls looking right at us. I could see them talking about us, for sure. That's why I wanted to leave when I did."

"Nervous, are you?" I said lightly.

"I don't like being discussed," he said sharply. "I've known them all for ages anyway; it must be big news, me being with a girl."

Liam sounded touchy, so I decided to leave it alone. I was growing familiar with a certain edge he had, and the subject of the two of us seemed to be right on that edge. *This part of Connemara must be a really small world,* I thought. *I'd be doing very well to consider that when it comes to Liam. It's his insular world, and there are things that matter to him within it that I have to be sensitive to because they're very real to him. The shame about it is I have to piece these things together through observation, watching as his moods change without prelude, and then trying to figure out exactly what had changed him.* I continued thinking it through, and realized Liam was a lot more sensitive than he let on. But then again, most people are.

I didn't say anything as we drove home. I figured Liam was still nursing his touchiness, but once we walked inside, he relaxed and made himself at home. He lit a fire and held out his hand for me to come and sit with him on the floor, as we had done before many times.

"Wait here, I'll be right back," Liam said. He went out to his car and came back carrying three books of poetry, from which he said he'd read if I promised to read my own poetry to him in return. He leaned back against the wall and read with slow deliberation from the works of Irish poets whose works I'd never heard read aloud. I watched Liam, thinking this was a rare quality in a man. I couldn't even listen to the poetry, so conscious was I of the way he read. *Irish poetry needs to be read in an Irish accent,* I thought. *It's a sacrilegious crime to hear it otherwise.*

Liam lay down the Patrick Kavanaugh book. "It's your turn now."

"What I write is different from that," I qualified. "I write about what's happening on the inside, either cerebrally or emotionally. I mean, everything I write is like an inner monologue, as opposed to an observation.

Many poets here seem to be talking about the landscape or the weather—you know, descriptive, tangible, external things." I was also thinking about the possibility of shocking Liam. Not that my poetry is so flagrantly shocking, it's just that it's revelatory, and I knew as a culture, the Irish were not the confessional sort when it comes to their emotions.

"Tell you what," I said. "I have a few here I'll let you take home; you can read them when I'm nowhere around. I don't think I'd be able to sit here and take the pressure of your scrutiny."

"Fair enough," Liam said, taking the poems from my hand and placing them aside.

There is such joy in newfound love once you have gone beyond the first stage. It's as if you can finally relax because something about it is so validating. Reciprocity is a narcissistic drug that keeps you coming back for more. So thick was the energy in the room between us that the hours fled without notice. So focused were we on each other that nothing in the world could have disturbed the mood and snapped me out of my revelry with the one exception of the next line Liam delivered. "Do you want me to stay?"

I moved out of my body and into my tangled mind abruptly. I'd been caught completely unaware. Of course this question was going to come up sooner or later, yet when it did, it was unexpected and I didn't have a ready response. I was doubtful and indecisive. Thus far, too much had seemed like a push and pull with Liam. More often than not, I couldn't tell what he was thinking, so I felt the need to be cautious. I couldn't reconcile my indecision because half of me did and half of me didn't want him to stay. What I really wanted was to get beyond the awkwardness of the moment to a place where the investment of time had developed my relationship with Liam a lot more than it had by this point. I thought there needed to be a much firmer foundation, which had to be incrementally earned. Anything else would be premature and I'm not the kind who goes jumping into anything without looking, I was still too uncertain, and when I'm uncertain, I don't move. I assumed I'd be certain one day; I just wasn't there yet. What surprised me was that he'd even asked the question in the first place. I was going to have to rise to the occasion and answer him.

"Not now," I said.

As he did in all things, Liam accepted my answer with immediate poise, but I was still able to rewind the moment and look at it in delay: his moment of hesitancy as he registered what I'd said, the stiffening of his body as he sat up taller and fixed me with his smile.

"Well, all right then," he said, and then he stood up and took my hand. We walked outside under the starlit night, weighed by the moment. Liam reached in his car and placed my poems in the passenger seat. He turned to hug me in a gesture of closure saying, "I'll be leaving in a few days for the musician's boat tour. We'll end up at Hughes at the end of the week, so you can come meet the boat at the Spiddal Pier if you want to. I'll be gone for a week, but I hope to see you before I go." I nodded and watched him get in the car, and then he flashed me a smile and drove into the night.

Chapter Eleven

The glass doors of my porch were screaming as they fought to abate the wind roaring inland from the sea. It woke me up earlier than usual and going to the window, I saw a blanket of dark clouds threatening a disastrous rain. As I prepared to meet the bus into Galway, I realized I had to time it perfectly, just as the bus was coming down the hill from Carraroe, or I'd be left standing unsheltered and impatient in the insistent rain.

I walked down to the coast road, grounding my feet heavily as the wind railed against my body, causing me to lean into it so it wouldn't knock me backward. There was no point in bringing my waxed hat or umbrella; both would only be blown to disuse the second I stepped outside. I'd seen these conditions before. I made it to my usual place across the street from the Centra, and stood expectantly until I noticed Mick Folan's van parked before the shop's door. Crossing the street, I intended to search for him, but he came swinging out of the shop and spotted me instantly. Long legs carrying him quickly forward, he thrust an arm across my shoulders and herded me into the shelter of the phone booth on the side of the road. Forcing the rattling door to an accordion fold, he pulled me inside.

"What in the world are you doing out in this? It's bitter cold," he said, drawing out the word bitter. "Where is it you think you're going?"

"I have to go into work," I told him.

"Well, you wouldn't want to be waiting for the bus out in this, so I'll take you meself," he said.

"Are you going into town?" I asked.

Claire Fullerton

"I am now." He reopened the phone booth door and made a dash to his van. I followed, tugging open the passenger door, and using all my strength to close it against the heinous wind.

"What I meant was, are you going into town anyway?" I tried again.

"And what I meant was, I am now," he said, with a level look that closed the subject.

He started the van and circled out of the lot in one fluid swing, leaving us pointed in the direction of Galway. I didn't say anything for a minute because I didn't know how to adequately thank him.

"I was just talking about you the other night to a guy I know named Patrick," I began.

"Were you now," he said.

"Yah, Patrick's a musician from New Zealand who's been here a couple of years from what I can tell. I think he, his two brothers, and sister all live in Spiddal."

"Ah," Mick said.

"Everyone in his family is a musician. Anyway, I think you two should meet. Seems Patrick is looking to expand his musical horizons, so I thought of you."

"Here you are playing the agent," he said. "You know, I've never had an agent."

"I don't know how much of an agent I am. I'm still trying to figure out how to get anything done in Ireland in general. When I figure that out, I'll take you on as a client, how about that?"

"You'll figure it out, all right," he said, as we passed the Connemara Hotel.

"So, what are you doing today besides picking up stranded travelers?" I asked.

"When she calms down, the Rainbow People are going to meet out in the bog."

"The Rainbow People? Who are they?"

"More like, what are they, really," he said. "I've been a member of the Rainbow People for two years now. We meet about helping the earth, preserving the beauty of Irish nature, and healing the planet," he said.

I listened intently. Very little of what Mick said ever surprised me.

"Ireland has always been a power point on the planet, you see—I told you that about Inverin, but it's true of all Ireland as well. Even though our land has been raped and starved in past generations, she's always regained her strength to heal her people. We Irish have a reciprocal relationship with the land. It's a give and take. The Rainbow People want to give to the land to help keep the balance. Tis' a symbiotic relationship, don't cha know."

"So, how does that happen? I mean, how does one give to the land?"

"We plant trees, shrubbery, flowers, anything she'll accept from us. We also assemble and pray. We pray for our land's health and such in a circle of ceremonial love. These things matter. We also tend to sacred sites, like the dolmen in the bog behind us. I think each gesture adds up. It's all about intention. Ireland's going to be coming back, now, her strength is rising," Mick said. "The Rainbow People is just a group involved."

It took little imagination for me to picture Mick doing this.

"It'll be a good world for Solas, so it will," he said definitively. I smiled my agreement.

"So, how's Gabrielle?" I switched the subject, realizing I hadn't seen Mick since the day he was at the Centra telling me he was leaving.

"I'll be picking her up from the bus at three thirty this afternoon. She's taking a photography class in town three days a week, now."

"All right, good for her," I said. "You know, when I last saw you, things were a bit shaky," I tested.

"Ah right, well, there's Solas now, and I have me responsibilities," Mick said. "Maybe it's all karmic with Gabe and I—don't know for sure. Maybe all these bits and pieces with her are meant to show me a bigger picture of something I need to learn. Then again, maybe I just don't understand ye women, is all."

"What don't you understand?" I laughed. "Tell me and I'll clear it all up."

"Well, you wouldn't be the one to know now, would you?" Mick said.

"Sure I would, I'm female."

"You are, yah, but it's not the same."

"How do you know? Anyway, what are you implying?"

"You're not trying to pin anyone down to hearth and home from what I can tell," Mick said, "doesn't seem you're the sort."

"What, you think that's what Gabrielle is trying to do?" I asked. "Is that what the problem is?"

"She surely is, and there's the struggle plain as day."

"Seems to me it's already happened, so she doesn't have to try, Mick," I said. "The two of you live under the same roof, have for some time now and you have a son together. What am I missing?"

"Just that she's needing me to be somebody I'm not." he said. "She's needing me to be here at this time, doing this at that time, and explaining meself when I'm not doing either to suit her. I'm just not any good at her expectations. I'm a free spirit, I'll tell you, and I aim to stay that way. I don't need any woman telling me what to do. All it makes me want to do is the opposite."

"Of course, I don't have all the facts, but maybe the conflict is in your definition of yourself as a free spirit," I said. "If you're so busy doing that, then you can't act naturally because you're too busy saying you're a free spirit. You might be blocking yourself. It's like you've got yourself so convinced you're a free spirit that you've painted yourself into a corner. The dynamic between you and Gabe is already contrary to that, because of the lifestyle you've got going, if you know what I mean. Maybe you should just adjust to it, become one with it. You're fighting against it instead. Must be exhausting."

Mick took a second and thought about it. "You've no doubt got something there; maybe we are working something out, Gabe and me. It's probably a soul lesson."

I cast a sidelong glance at Mick, thinking there was something about him I took absolutely seriously. Most people don't go around instigating this kind of conversation out of nowhere, but Mick's mind was always out there looking for deeper meaning. Every conversation I ever had with him was layered with poignancy because he was just coming from a different space from everyone else, and few people are so readily forthright. He always seemed to have the big picture in mind, or he was rarely far from it. It gave me the opportunity to consider my own vantage point, the way meaningful friendships do.

"I think we're being helped through life, Hailey, I really do. It's more than karma and soul lessons: it's a greater divinity, and divinity is all around us—has been since the beginning of time, and always will be. It's not only in a few places, in a few churches, or in a few books. It's everywhere. We don't even have to look very hard; we just have to understand it's there. The only question we have to ask ourselves is 'where are we?'"

"Get back to you and Gabrielle; I mean, what's your point?" I wanted to hear how it tied in.

"Okay, here's my point: the way of nature is diverse and roundabout like that stream that runs through the bog. If you have an aerial view, the stream runs straight, and then turns and in some parts, it's completely hidden from view if you're standing beside it. Eventually, you can see it resurface, yet you never can gainsay where it's going, now can you? But there's a destination; there's a plan. It's just like our lives. We can't see the plan because we're living in the middle of it while things unfold. Our lives are like the flowing stream. I think we all have our destinations. The things that happen to us along the way are part of the unfolding toward our destiny.

"Relationships are a part of it. We learn from relationships, mostly we learn about ourselves, but they are part of the hidden process of things. I feel like that sometimes with Gabrielle, like I'm in this with her to learn something. So, on the one hand, I think something important is at hand, and on the other, I want to get the upper hand and control everything because I'm human. I'm watching the flow, and trying to conduct it at the same time. That could be what the conflict is. I will say this: there is no more important place in the world than the arena of human relationships. It's where we learn everything."

"Everything about ourselves, or everything about each other?" I asked.

"Both," Mick said.

"All right, if you're watching the flow, in a way you're also conducting. You're creating things as you go along, aren't you?" I asked. "I mean, which comes first?"

"They're one and the same because I'm co-creating," he clarified.

"All right, you're co-creating," I complied.

"Yah, I'm co-creating with God, and the struggle concerns letting God lead. I think it's enough just to try. Anyway, I think that's what's going on between Gabe and me."

"That's a great take on things Mick," I said. It seemed the air lightened from the conclusion of Mick's point. I stared out the van window, watching the changing coastline into Galway.

"It's a fine woman who can keep up with the likes of me," Mick said.

"Seems to me Gabrielle does a pretty good job at that," I returned.

"I wasn't talking about Gabe; I was talking about you," he said. Even though I was flattered, I deflected the compliment because I've never known how to take one.

"I think the thing to do is just take it easy on Gabrielle. She probably doesn't understand things the same way you do," I said.

"I don't think she does either," Mick said. "She's French; she's earthier, don'tcha know. Anyway, that's sound advice," he nodded. "Listen, I want you to bring your guitar around. Let's have a lesson soon," Mick said, as we passed through Salthill.

"I'd love to. I haven't touched it in months because I don't know how to play it. It's just been sitting in the corner of my living room. That guitar belonged to my older brother," I said.

"Well, bring her round, and let's have a look at her."

"I'll do that. Thank you so much for the ride, Mick; that was really nice of you, I appreciate it."

"Not at all," he said. "You'd do the same for me."

"I would," I said, as we turned on New Road.

I got out of the car in the courtyard and ran headlong

against the thrashing rain until I pushed through the Centre's door. I turned, waved to Mick, and ducked inside. The wind slammed the Centre's door loudly behind me. I peeled out of my coat and shook it, snapping off the rain.

"Good God, I can't believe this weather," I said, looking at Shannon, Darren, and Declan, who were leisurely drinking tea in the downstairs room.

"She's pissing rain," Darren said sternly.

"Ah, none of you cowboys can take a little weather," Declan stated, with a note of superiority.

"What's going on?" I hung my coat on the nail by the door.

"Declan just fired Adrian," Shannon said succinctly.

"What?" I was taken aback.

"You can't fire someone who's not earning a wage," Darren said to Shannon.

"You know what I mean," Shannon said, looking at me.

"Lookit," Declan heated up defensively. "I didn't fire anybody. We just don't need Adrian hanging around here all the time; all I did was tell him that." I could tell this conversation had been going on for a while, and the wind had unwittingly blown me right into the middle of it.

"Who's he hurting?" Shannon sounded like she'd asked the question before.

"Are his feelings hurt?" I cut through to Shannon.

"Oh, his poor feelings!" whined Declan, theatrically.

"Of course," Shannon said.

"Oooh," Declan continued, rubbing his eyes with his fists and thrusting out his lower lip.

"Declan, cut it out." Shannon glared at Declan with a look that could have cut through steel.

"Youse two are too soft," he said. "Pansies, the pair

of youse."

"I'm going out for a fag. I can't take this." Darren stood up and stretched.

"Yah, and you can light one for me in the pouring rain, will ye," said Declan as Darren walked out, slamming the door. A second later, Declan sprang up and followed him.

"Well." Shannon stood up and started walking upstairs. I followed, pulling out the chair beneath the computer table while she picked up the phone.

"What are you doing?" I asked.

"Calling Adrian."

"When did he leave?"

"About a half hour ago. You just missed it."

I waited as Shannon left a message with Adrian's mother.

"Please tell him to call Shannon and Hailey at the Centre," she said.

"Nice woman." She set the phone in its cradle and turned to me. "His mother says he might be in town. She'll find him and give him the message. I think we should take Adrian to lunch."

"What an American thing to do," I said laughing. "Do Irish people know how to do lunch?"

"Come on, Hailey," she said although the smile on her face told me she got the joke. "I feel sorry for the guy."

"I do, too. Adrian's probably not going to want to call here in case Declan answers," I said.

"Adrian doesn't think that way, trust me," Shannon said, and she was right. Adrian called the Centre an hour later, and it was I who answered the phone.

"Hailey, how's the form?" Adrian asked when I picked up the phone.

"How's the form yourself, Adrian?"

"You've no doubt heard the news that I've been fired?" he said.

"Yah, I heard you've been fired." I looked straight at Shannon.

"Ask him if he wants to meet us at Le Graal," she whispered.

"Do you want to meet Shannon and me at Le Graal?"

"That would be grand," Adrian said. I nodded at Shannon.

"Ask him what time."

"What time?"

"Half one," he said.

"Okay," I nodded toward Shannon. "We'll see you there."

"Half one," I repeated, hanging up the phone.

Shannon and I walked out the Centre's door a little after one o' clock, and thankfully, the rain had fully stopped. On the way to meet Adrian, we stopped in Paul Neumans' antique shop, for lack of a better description, and browsed around the odds and ends in the little, one-room shop on Mill Street called the Dragon's Lair. Paul's door was always open; it was hard to pass by without stepping in. For no particular reason, I bought a circular, gray ceramic plaque that depicted a scene from the Book of Kells. It had three ominous-looking dogs holding each other's tails in their mouths in a perfect circle surrounded by Celtic interlacing.

"Where are you going to put that?" Shannon asked with an edge of doubt in her voice.

"I don't know. It's not like it goes with anything." I turned it over in my hands. "What's it going to do, interrupt the thematic decor I've got going on in Inverin?"

"Good point," Shannon said.

We started again toward Dominick Street and within seconds, we ran right into Kieran Murphy. I was glad to see Kieran because there was something so pleasing about him. He was always smiling, and charming, and every time I saw him, I marveled at the striking resemblance he had to the actor Mel Gibson. The three of us stopped short at the sight of each other. We exchanged pleasantries, commented on the weather, and then Kieran addressed me.

"I heard Liam was looking for you the other night," he said.

"When?" I didn't know which night he meant.

"The other night when Leigh McDonough played in town." Kieran smiled widely.

I smiled back as if it would help me get the point. I didn't have a clue what he was talking about; I thought he must be confused. I was just glad Kieran and I could discuss Liam so easily, for every time I saw him, I thought of the night I had first met Liam and of Kieran's embarrassing involvement. Kieran gave me a huge grin, as if there were some inside joke we shared.

"I'm not sure what you're talking about," I finally said.

"I heard Liam went into the lesbian bar, where Leigh was playing, looking for you." His eyes twinkled with mirth.

"When was this?" I glanced at Shannon, who stood poker-faced like she always did, following the conversation.

"Friday night," Kieran intoned, as if it should have been obvious.

I quickly thought back, and it dawned on me that was the night I was with Deanna Rader after work. That was also the night Liam went out of his way not to ask me to explain.

"How do you know that?" I asked, considering his source of information probably made a difference.

"One of the girls I know from Spiddal was there in the club when Liam came in," he said. "She saw Liam walk through the door."

One of the girls from Spiddal implied one of the women who had grown up with Liam, as in, one of the girls who had a right to keep tabs on him and pass around her findings because Liam was a member of her own tribe. This was the kind of thing that made Liam nervous.

"Why did she tell you?" I asked.

"Because she thought it was funny. Think about it: your man walks into a place looking for his girl because he doesn't know where she is, and he's trying to track her down—he doesn't even know he's in a lesbian bar!" he exhaled the joke. "She went straight to the door when she saw him and told him he was in the wrong place. I think she wanted to save him the embarrassment of walking further into the room. It's great fun. Anyway, everybody knows about it," he added. His ear-to-ear smile told me he enjoyed having something on Liam, and it was making him pleasantly puffed up with himself, or, as they say in Ireland, it was making him "chuffed."

"I don't know anything about that," I said.

"He must really fancy you," Kieran concluded.

I felt warmed at the sound of that, but I also felt strangely defensive on Liam's behalf. Because I was glaringly aware of just how much Liam liked to keep things private, I didn't like the fact he was being discussed any more than he would have, so I changed the subject. I told Kieran we were on our way to meet someone "up the road," which is the standard Irish way of saying where we're going is none of your business.

Shannon and I walked away from Kieran until she finally shared her thoughts.

"This is big," she said.

"What?" I said, distractedly.

"Prince Charming," she said.

"All right, let's talk about this." I stopped and turned to her.

I loved talking to Shannon because as an American, I liked to think she saw things from my perspective, that she spoke the same language from a similar vantage point, and she could therefore be counted on to serve as the accurate voice of reason.

"So, the night I was with Deanna doing nothing in general, Liam went to my house and I wasn't there," I began.

"So he drove into Galway looking for you," Shannon added.

"Right." I resumed walking toward Le Graal.

"And, as if he wasn't in torment enough because you weren't home, he goes looking for you in town and runs into someone who knows him," Shannon continued.

"Who asks him what he's doing because he's clearly in the wrong place."

"Which is news enough because it's a lesbian bar, and then he says he's looking for you," she said.

"Weird he didn't know what kind of a place it was," I pondered aloud. "This is Galway; it's not like he didn't grow up around here."

"The boy must not get out enough."

"Somebody should have told Toto he wasn't in Kansas."

Shannon laughed, continuing. "So, the fact that he was out of his element isn't the news. The news is he was caught looking for you. This is big."

"This is big," I repeated.

"Everybody knows!" Shannon yelled effusively in her best imitation of Kieran's accent.

We walked through the front room of Le Graal looking for Adrian, yet couldn't find him. The whole of the dark wine bar is made of two adjoining rooms, so we continued onward, passing the bar at our right until we reached the fireplace at the back wall where we spotted Adrian. He was settled at a table in front of the fire with a cup of tea and a notebook, sitting at ease as if he'd been there a while.

I'd never seen the inside of Le Graal in the daytime since it's the kind of place people go to primarily at night. The most sophisticated of musical acts passing through Galway perform in front of the fire in the back room, and there is a feel to its candlelit interior like that of a literary den infused with jewel-toned, overstuffed seating arrangements. There is a seriousness to Le Graal that cannot be found in any other establishment in Galway. People go there when they want the mood more formal, when romance might be an issue, or when they want to exchange the culturally ingrained habit of porter for the novelty of a good glass of wine. Shannon and I sat down at Adrian's table.

"Thank you for calling me," Adrian began.

"Glad to do it." Shannon looked quickly from Adrian to me.

"Adrian," I cut to the chase, "why don't you tell me what happened."

"I don't know what happened, it's just Declan is all." He took off his round-lens glasses and set them on his notebook.

"He was in a mood this morning," Shannon continued, looking at me. "You should have seen him; he was all wound up over who knows what."

"He didn't have to take it out on me," Adrian said.

"Exactly what did he say?" I had known better than to ask Declan, who would have only given a litany of justification.

"He said I was hanging around the Centre for no reason, and it was just best if I didn't, like. I should be out working for a living, doing something with meself, that sort of thing."

"His commentary on your life, right?" I said.

"Right, Hailey. According to Declan, I haven't the sense to figure these things out for meself."

"I don't think Declan sees how much Hailey and I need you," Shannon interjected, and the whole tenor of the conversation was set on coarse. Although I knew Shannon had overstated it, I acknowledged the kindness in her sentiment and was touched by its appropriateness. Sometimes people can say the perfect thing at the right time, and this was one of them.

Shannon swiveled to her left, and I turned to see Darren approach with his squinting eyes adjusting, sweeping the room. Shannon walked toward him, then the two came to the table hand in hand.

"I'm going to have to go a little early," Shannon said. "Do you remember Bernard saying he has a line on a drum kit for the Centre? I'm going with Darren to talk to the guy about it."

"The music shop is just up the road; we better get on it if we're going to be renting out the rehearsal space," Darren explained. "Adrian, are you well?"

"Well enough, indeed," came Adrian's reply. "I like this about the kit, Bernard seems to always have friends in high places."

"He does," I said. "Why is that? It doesn't matter what's going on in Galway, Bernard knows about it."

"He grew up in Galway. His family is old Galwegian, and when Bernard was coming up, Galway was a lot smaller. It was easier to get around, easier to know everyone," Darren said.

"He's a good guy to have on our side," I noted. "Most landlords don't care what goes on in the space they're renting, but Bernard seems to legitimately care about the Centre. Nice guy."

"Respectable chap," Darren agreed.

"It helps that he lives in front of the courtyard," Shannon said. "That way he sees what we're doing with all the people coming and going. I think it'd impress anyone."

"He can keep an eye on us as well," said Darren. "You know, make sure we're not up to anything untoward."

"Yah, right," Adrian said. "What gets me is for some reason Bernard seems to take Declan seriously."

"I don't know about that," I said, "Every time I see Bernard talking to Declan, he has a look on his face like he's sizing him up."

"Searching for what he's hiding, more like it," Darren corrected.

"He's right to be keeping an eye on the place, he does own the property," Shannon pointed out.

"Bernard said we should call up to your man immediately." Darren took Shannon's hand. "We're away, then. Nice to see you both."

"Adrian, will I see you later?" Shannon said over her shoulder.

"Not at the Centre," he said quickly.

"Hey, look, we'll work something out." I looked up at Shannon. "See you two later. Good luck."

I was left with Adrian to pick up the conversation. "I have to tell you something, Hailey. The Centre was more than just a place to hang out: it was a place for me to go every day, to get me out of the house, don't cha know."

"I understand," I said, following along.

"You see, I'm a wee depressed at times. Sometimes more so than others, like. Some days I don't want to leave me bed all day, and nothing in the world can make me otherwise." I took him at his word and knew he wasn't finished.

"The Centre made me feel involved with something and it was a good thing. I know I wasn't coming up with plans, or taking on musicians the way you do, but I felt good about being there should the two of youse have needed me. I told me ma I was working for two American ladies."

"I am honored," I said. My sympathy was building, weighing heavily on my chest.

"I don't know what I'm going to be doing now. My father needs me to help on the farm, but that would mean getting up every morning at four and by nature, I'm not suited for it."

"Getting up at four and doing what?" I was curious. For some reason, Adrian didn't appear to be the farm type—I just couldn't picture him working the land or whatever else it is people do on an Irish farm.

"Seeing the sheep out to pasture, clearing the land, that kind of thing."

"Where exactly do you live, Adrian?"

"Carnakelly, Athenry," he said, "but we have a wee flat here in town as well. It's not much, mind you, just a place to hang me hat, but I've stayed there these past few months. I've been going home only on the weekends."

I sat putting the pieces together so that I had a better understanding. I knew so little of Adrian outside of what I'd seen of him at the Centre. Also, I was always intrigued to hear anything about the way people lived in rural Ireland because it was not something they readily volunteered. When you first meet someone in Ireland, it may feel as if you've known them forever because they're so easygoing and seemingly accessible, but it is only a mask. The reality is the Irish reveal precious little about themselves to outsiders, so it takes a while to ferret out what's really going on until you win their trust.

"Adrian, it might not all be bad news, this business of Declan firing you," I said. I looked for a way to try to explain. "I worked for a guy named Alan Koslowski in Los Angeles a while back. He is a very spiritual man, a very wise man. I remember one time he decided to let an employee go. He said he was actually liberating the guy to move on to other things. I'll never forget that. It just stayed with me the way things do when you know there's an element of truth involved. Alan's point was that it's all in the way you consider things; I'm inclined to agree with him. For all we know, Declan could have done you the biggest favor imaginable because now there's a new path before you. If you keep an open mind, you'll see you're free to start again."

"Yah, but I don't know what I'm going to do, I can't figure out what I'm good at," Adrian confessed.

"Sure you do, Adrian. Just look at what you're naturally good at doing. Take a look at what motivates you, what interests you, what makes your heart sing," I encouraged. "We've all got something somewhere."

"Well, I'm a bit of a poet," he said.

"There you go."

"Not much money in that. The only good poet is a dead poet," he added.

"Don't be ridiculous, Adrian, money isn't the point. It's not about money. You simply have to understand that your only obligation is to be true to yourself and carry on from there. Incidentally, I'd love to read some of your poetry."

"Fair enough," he said. "I'll ring you one day and bring some out."

"Well, I don't have a phone out in Inverin, but you can always call me at the Centre. Anyway, I think you should still come by every so often and visit. You know how capricious Declan can be: what he says one day, he changes the next."

"I've noticed," he said, smiling from the opportunity to take a jab at Declan.

"Just don't feel like you can't come around. Wait a little while until Declan gets over it. I wouldn't take the situation too seriously if I were you, all right? Let's just see what pans from here."

"All right," he said. "I should be going now, anyway. I've met a new girl. I'm going to take her out driving on my motorcycle."

"You move on to other things quicker than I gave you credit for, Adrian."

"Yah, well, a man's gotta do what he's gotta do," he said definitively.

"Just make sure you continue to remember that." I got up with him to leave.

We walked out into the street together, where Adrian got on his motorcycle and slowly drove away.

Back at the Centre, Shannon and I made no mention of Adrian, lest we get Declan all riled again. After I took the last bus to Inverin, I entered my porch to discover a dozen long-stemmed tiger lilies wrapped in coral-colored paper on the doorstep. My heart leaped—*Of course they're from Liam; he's making some gesture over the other night, who knew he had it in him?* I thought, tearing open the attached envelope. I placed the lilies on the kitchen counter and hastily scanned the card:

"Thank you for everything, love Adrian," the card read. The kindness of the gesture usurped any disappointment I might have had that the flowers were not from Liam. I was so touched by Adrian, it almost broke my heart.

I looked at the flowers, looked at the clock, and wondered if Liam would appear at some point during the next few hours. I never knew what he was going to do. If he did show up, I considered his reaction to the vase of flowers standing prominently on the counter. If he were true to form, he'd go out of his way to hide his curiosity. I'd seen him censor himself many times before, and for some reason, it amused me. I decided I'd volunteer absolutely nothing for the sheer sport of watching him censor himself again. I remembered he'd be leaving in a few days for the boat tour, and that he'd asked me to be at the Spiddal Pier on Sunday. I wondered if I would see him before he left; if not, it'd be a week before I did. Next, I worried because I was worrying about it too much, and because Liam never did appear that night, I worried up until eleven o'clock, and then I turned myself off and went on to bed.

Chapter Twelve

The next day, I went to work at the Centre. It was an unremarkable day beyond the fact there had been no mention of Adrian and no word from Liam. When my thoughts turned to Liam, the disquieting stirrings of doubt and uncertainty rumbled within me. I told myself what I didn't know wouldn't hurt me, that no news was good news, and I became a study in annoying, placating platitudes. *Why is it,* I wondered, *the second you begin to let somebody in, you give them the power to wreak havoc on your peace of mind?*

At the end of the day, I went back to Inverin and took a long walk through the bog to clear my head, but the minute I returned, I became unsettled all over again, wondering why Liam had suddenly changed the dynamic. Not knowing what was going on was really starting to bother me, so I took my journal onto the porch and started writing, hoping it would soothe the troubling energy. I looked up at the sounds of a car scratching up the driveway. Seconds later, Liam slid open the door and stepped in with an air of cool indifference there was no way I could've missed.

"Hiya," Liam said, as if he had seen me ten minutes earlier. "I was just down the road at the Cruiscan and am on my way home; I thought I'd stop in for a second."

Okay, I thought, *I get it: this means you're not staying.*

"Are you playing tonight?" I asked, knowing full well he was.

"Yah, at ten thirty, are you going to be there?"

Okay, I thought, *I get this: he's not asking me to*

come with him, he's asking me if I'm going to be sitting there in the crowd watching him—as if he's just curious. What's he doing?

"Well, I wasn't planning on it," I said with the emphasis on the word planning. "Maybe I will."

"Oh no, that's okay," he said, then without saying another word, he walked out to his car and returned with the sunglasses I'd left behind.

"Here." Liam placed them on the table. "Well, I won't be seeing you for a week or so because I'm leaving tomorrow."

"I know," I said, "you'll be going on the boat from port to port."

"We'll be coming in Sunday night to play Hughes. We'll be at the Spiddal Pier around nine; there'll be a lot of people there. Come if you want," he said. "If not, I'll see you another time."

Why is he being so casual? I thought. *What is this; invasion of the body snatchers? Who took his personality? Is he trying to appear cool, or does he legitimately mean this? Why do I think this is an act?*

I just nodded because I was starting to get the picture, and was thinking indifference should be met with indifference. Not only that, he was starting to get on my nerves. "All right, have a good time," I said.

"See ya," Liam said, and then he walked out the door.

Oddly, the next morning I felt a wave of relief wash over me. I was so grateful that I decided to jump right into the middle of it so that it would stay. There was no need to think about Liam anymore because he was gone and wouldn't be back for days. If this was going to be confusing, then I was going to be bigger than my confusion. Maybe I wasn't the one who was confused after all, maybe it was Liam, and I was only being drawn into his confusion. Whichever was the case, I didn't have to think about him for a while and I was glad.

I did a double take out the bus window as it approached its only routine stop in the center of Spiddal, right across the street from the Cruiscan at the front door of a little boutique hotel. There he was again, that same man I'd seen at this stop a couple of times before. He would have stood out conspicuously anywhere, with his willowy elegant, five-feet-nine inch frame and his round blue eyes in a face devoid of time. A derby hat topped his alabaster hair, and he levied a slim black walking stick one pace before him, as if he were posing for a photograph. He wore a white buttoned-down shirt with a tailored gray suit, and his black leather shoes were polished to an impressive shine. The last time I'd seen him, I wondered what a man dressed like that was doing on the western coast of Ireland. I watched furtively as he entered the bus, nodding to the people on board who returned his nod readily with a dose of respect as he made his way down the aisle and sat lightly on the seat beside me.

"Nice day," he said to me, drawing a hand to his hat, which he tapped once with a salutary dip of his head.

I was learning how to respond the Irish way. "It is, yah," I returned quickly.

"American, are you?"

"I am, yah."

"From the South, is it?"

"That's a good ear you have. Memphis, Tennessee," I said. "But there were also the last five years spent in Los Angeles. Now I'm here."

"God helps us all." He winked. I got the joke. "What's your name, then?" he said, studying me.

"Hailey Crossan," I said.

"Have you any Irish connections?"

"Yes," I said. "On both of my parents' sides. Everyone, in fact, was either Scottish or Irish."

"So, you're not all bad then," he said with a broad, small-toothed smile.

"Only some of the time, in spite of my Irish connections."

"My name's Kearney," he said. "Seamus Kearney. Pleased to meet you."

"Nice to meet you, too."

"What's your middle name, then?" he continued. I got the impression he was really trying to classify me.

"Ford," I said.

"Two last names, is it? Odd for a girl."

"Well maybe, I'm not an odd girl though; I promise I'm all right."

"The Fords, now, they're Irish as the soil," he said, seeming satisfied to finally categorize me. "They're from these parts," he said.

"That's what I understand, but I didn't know that until I came to Connemara."

"So, they called you to come here, did they?"

"Well, no, it was just a whim that brought me here really. I believe all of my relatives are dead. I never met any of them," I said, hoping that cleared it up.

"So, they called you here, did they?" he repeated patiently, his brow rose as if coaxing me to comply.

"Yes, definitely," I said.

"There are Fords in the graveyard right beside my house," he said.

"Oh really? Which graveyard?"

"We just passed it. You know the road to the Spiddal Pier? The one by the church?"

"Yes," I said.

"My house is next to the church, across from the boys' school, there."

"I didn't know that was a school," I said. I had noticed a series of nondescript gray stone buildings set back from the road, but I never knew what they were used for.

"Ah, yah. Used to be a hospital before that. That's where the name Spiddal comes from. Think of the word Spiddal and you can hear the word hospital in it. This area was a hospital area long ago. This is the area where the sick were healed."

"I didn't know that."

"Oh yes. Now then, there are Fords up the road there in the other graveyard as well," he said.

"Which one?" I asked, although it immediately hit me there was only one other graveyard in the area.

"The one by the Centra, there," he said, confirming my thought.

"I know where that is. What's interesting is there are only a handful of names in that graveyard, but there are so many buried there."

"It's the region," he said. "You have Connolly, Keneely, Folan, Flaherty, Hennessey, Burke, bit of your name of course, all old names. You're right, not many more names way out there."

"Hennessey, that's a name I hear around here often," I said.

"Ah, you must know the boys, then."

"I do, a little," I said, understating things.

"Which one?"

"I know Liam." I started thinking I probably shouldn't be saying even that, but I couldn't help myself.

"The box player," he said. "Nice boy, talented one, so

he is."

I switched the subject quickly.

"Do you always dress like that?" I asked.

"Like what?" He seemed completely unaware. I tried to hide my embarrassment, wondering if I'd put my foot in my mouth.

"You look so nice. I was only thinking that."

"Pride of person, not an unpardonable sin," he said. "Going into town, are you, where you go every day?"

Nothing gets by anybody around here, I thought.

"Yes. I work at the Galway Music Centre on New Road."

"Tell me all about it," Seamus leaned back, getting comfortable as we progressed toward Galway.

The next thing I knew, I was explaining everything we did at the Centre, while Seamus gave me his rapt attention with a pleased look on his face. Had I still been in Los Angeles, a conversation like the one I was having with Seamus Kearney would never have taken place. One simply did not divulge information to strangers in LA without thinking it could come back to haunt in some unexpected way. The bus rolled to a stop at the Spanish Arch in Galway. I stood up, ready to disembark.

"Nice to meet you, Mr. Kearney," I said sincerely.

"Seamus, please. Nice to meet you, Hailey Ford Hennessey." He smiled up at me.

I stopped stock-still and looked at him; then I put one foot in front of the other. His parting line stayed with me for the rest of the day.

When I walked into the Centre, Declan immediately called a meeting. The four of us clamored upstairs to the loft, where Declan picked up his guitar and started strumming. I shot a look at Shannon, who shrugged her shoulders in silent reply to the question on my face.

Darren sat with his legs crossed, waiting.

"Right, then," Declan began. "I want to talk to youse."

We all stared at him expectantly. Just then, the front door downstairs opened.

"Hiya," came a voice questioningly. "Declan are you in there?"

"Owen?" Declan called back. In Declan's Derry accent, the name Owen came out sounding more like "Ohn." "We're up here starting a meeting," he called down.

"I'll wait," Owen said.

Declan repositioned his chair, facing us straight on. "Right," he began again.

The door downstairs banged closed loudly. Declan jumped to his feet without a word and ran down the stairs in a burst of energy. The three of us remained where we were.

"I'm going to get a cup of tea," Darren said, rising to walk downstairs.

"Declan's going to talk to us about money," Shannon said, turning to face me.

"How do you always know everything?" I asked.

"Declan can't keep things to himself for long. So, how's Prince Charming?"

"Don't ask," I said.

"You still going to meet him on Sunday?"

"I don't know, I haven't decided. Actually, I kind of doubt it."

"Leigh has a show at the Roisin Dubh Sunday night. Declan wants to have us all out to his house before the show so he can cook some Chinese thing I've never heard of. Did you know Declan used to work in his parents' Chinese restaurant in Derry before he came to Galway?"

"No," I said.

"It's really his mother's restaurant. I think Declan used to manage it."

"Imagine that," I said without inflection.

Darren walked up the stairs carrying four cups of tea and within seconds, we heard the door open and close again. Declan appeared at the top of the stairs.

"Right," he said, sitting down in his chair, reaching for a cup of tea. "I want us to do two things: I want to call out to James B. Farrell and Silas Burke of the arts council to see about getting a grant for the Centre. We have to keep trying for funding."

"This will be the third time we've done this," Shannon reminded us.

"We have to meet with Silas Burke. He holds an open forum in the lobby of Jury's hotel once a month. All we have to do is put our name on the list and wait to meet with him. Hailey can come with me," Declan said.

"I'm not an Irish citizen," I pointed out. "That might look kind of weird."

"We can chat to him about your citizenship too," Declan said. "Lookit, the *Advertiser* is going to call out here to do a piece on us. Even they know we're doing something here. I think we have a right to call out and tell Silas Burke just that."

"All right, I'll go with you," I said. "When is it?"

"Saturday week," he said.

"A week from Saturday." Shannon looked at me, translating.

"I know," I said, more defensively than I intended.

"So what's Owen doing here?" Darren looked at Declan.

"Obviously checking on his investment," Shannon answered.

"I've got it under control," Declan said with full bravado. "Youse don't have to worry about that."

"Did you tell him we're going to be getting a rehearsal room together?" I asked.

"I did, yah," said Declan. "I want to advertise about that as soon as possible. When the *Advertiser* calls out, we'll be sure to mention it. It'll be like free advertising for us."

"Now that we have the drum kit, we can get started on the room downstairs," Darren said. "We'll get it built in no time; I already have the PA. Since the musicians bring their own gear, there's not much else we'll need to do."

"Except keep a schedule of bookings, but Hailey and I can do that," Shannon said.

"This will be day and night, right?" I asked.

"Oh yah," Darren said. "It has to be."

"Do we have to be here overseeing the rehearsals or what?" I wanted to know.

"No, not at all," Declan jumped in. "I'll chat to Bernard. He can let people in and lock up after they leave since he's just right here."

"Well, we can try it that way, but if it's a hassle for Bernard, we're probably going to have to just keep it to days," I said.

"It'll be fine. I think the room will be used mostly at night anyway," Declan said.

"Probably right on that," said Darren. "It's easier to get together at night, some people work during the day."

Darren was right. Within the week, the rehearsal room was in full operation because word on the street was all it took. The energy of the Galway Music Centre began to change from that point onward as more and more musicians flowed through our door. There was always the steady throb of bass guitar rocking the floor upstairs, and it accompanied every minute of the day while the four of us continued to meet with musicians, book them into clubs, organize their press kits and introduce them to each other. Musicians living in Galway, as well as musicians living on the outskirts of town, came to the Centre regularly because we were the only rehearsal space in town, and the room blossomed into a steady source of income that catapulted the Centre into a viable local business unlike any other in Galway.

Chapter Thirteen

I was so glad to have an excuse not to be at the Spiddal Pier when Liam's boat came in that I dove at the opportunity to be anywhere else. Things had been too weird the last time I'd seen Liam, so I had gone gratefully to Declan's house. From there, all of us went to The Roisin Dubh to hear Leigh McDonough play before a sold-out crowd. The night ended at eleven thirty, and I returned home cautiously, half expecting to find Liam somewhere on the premises when I arrived. I braced myself in case he was, and was disappointed when he was not.

I didn't know exactly what was up, but I knew conditions had changed with Liam and I hadn't seen it coming. I wasn't sure if I should respond in kind to Liam's nonchalance, or if that would only exacerbate things; all I knew was I cared about it tremendously. I thought about the conversation Liam had instigated that night in Hughes wherein he'd asked me what I thought about rejection. I felt good about what I'd said in response, but it didn't happen to be the exact truth. What I really think about rejection is that it invites self-defense. Even the mere suggestion of rejection causes the person on the receiving end to start guarding against further insult, just in case it's really going to be bad. I didn't want to discuss rejection with Liam, I wanted him to lighten up so we could just continue along without having to analyzing everything.

Two days later, I stood looking out the window, noticing the days were growing shorter as they led into the third week of October. At a quarter till five, the sun had already reached its total decline. Out of the corner of my eye, I saw Liam's car turn into the driveway. I walked outside and stood on the wall that delineates the driveway from the yard. The light from the porch cast a flood on the grass, and Liam walked into its circle like an actor walking on stage.

"I was just in the neighborhood," Liam began.

"How was your tour?" I gestured for him to come into the living room.

"Long and often times wet. It rained practically every time we pulled out of port, but eventually the sun came out." He took off his jacket and sat down.

"How many places did you play, five?"

"Actually, seven. There was a festival in Clare where we played two pubs in one night. You've been to Clare, have you?" he asked.

"Yes. I've been as far as Doolin."

"So, you've been to Kinvara along the way?"

"Yes. Declan took Shannon and me when Shannon's sister came over from Washington, D.C., about three months ago. Nice little port town. There was a festival there at the time, something about a boat race."

"That must have been the hooker races. We call those boats hookers now, but they're just like the old currachs used at sea in generations past. Anyway, we played Kinvara last Saturday night," he said.

The conversation took on a life of its own, and no reference to the last time we'd seen each other was ever made. It crossed my mind that Liam had not thought twice about it, which meant he was probably unaware of how he had presented himself. He stayed chatting amiably for two hours before he slowly got up to leave.

"I'd like to ask you out for this Thursday." He rose from his chair. "On a date," he added, eyeing me for my reaction.

This may have something to do with the night he came here and I wasn't home, I thought.

"There's a classical trio from London that will be playing at NUI, you know, National University Ireland in Galway. They're called the Rogere Trio. It starts at seven if you're available."

"All right, that will be great," I said.

"We can meet at Taaffes after you leave work, if you'd like."

"Okay, do you want to say five thirty?"

"Okay." He paused. "You haven't even noticed I got some sun on my face. My mother says I got a little color out there at sea."

"I can see that, it looks good," I said, wondering at his disappointed tone of voice.

After Liam left, I considered what he was really saying to me. For a split second, he looked like a pouting little kid. I had the impression I should have praised him somehow, just as his mother had done, but since I had not, I was guilty of not measuring up to his mother's standard, which I thought was weird. Maybe I'd had it all wrong: for all of his purported nonchalance, maybe Liam really had expectations. I was pretty sure he'd been turning something over in his head that involved me, but I had no way of knowing what it was. It seemed to me he was trying to find his footing. *Too bad this young man didn't arrive with some kind of manual,* I thought.

On Thursday afternoon, I walked up Shop Street toward Taaffes wearing my long black coat against the changing Irish season. I pushed open the door and saw Liam and Patrick in front of the glowing fire. Both stood up when they saw me, then Liam stepped forward and gallantly kissed me on both sides of my face.

Uncharacteristic bold move in front of his friend; this is a first, I thought. *I wonder if this will fall under the category of "everybody's going to know."* Liam handed me a Guinness while he and Patrick resumed the conversation they were having before I walked in. It seemed they were strategizing the logistics of how Patrick could see his parents, who had recently come to town from New Zealand, without running into his brothers and sister since they had yet to settle their quarrel.

"So the way I see it, I can do everything on the sly," Patrick said. "I can call out to Spiddal when Steve's not there and set up a time to meet for a pint at the Cruiscan, and to hell with the lot of the rest of them."

"The lot of the rest of them? I asked. "What, this has gotten bigger?"

"Patrick's really sinking his teeth into this one," Liam said.

"I am, yah; I'm having a four-course meal. This is a matter of principle," Patrick said, but he was smiling.

"Don't ever make a Kiwi mad," Liam interjected.

"Wouldn't dream of it," I said.

"Your man's right. Every last one of us will make fair game of drama," Patrick laughed.

I shook my head, telling Patrick it all seemed complicated to me before Liam and I said goodbye and began the chilled, dark cobblestoned walk across town to NUI in a wind that knew no mercy.

The campus of National University Ireland in Galway is magnificent with its local limestone construction and Tudor Gothic design. It sits majestically on the banks of the River Corrib like a venerable shrine to higher learning centered on a well-tended quadrangle that harkens back to its mid-eighteen hundreds inception. The Rogere Trio performed in an acoustically perfect room with arched doorways and a thirty-foot-high vaulted ceiling, spinning royal magic from the union of a violin, cello, and grand piano.

Stealing a glance at Liam, I thought I'd never seen anyone so enraptured. He seemed to meld with the movements with his eyes closed, joining in wavelike: one musician understanding another with a sense of patriotic camaraderie so blissfully tangible I could feel the music's fluidity. I didn't dare disturb his otherworldly stillness until the performance was over; it was many heartbeats later before he emerged from his trance. When it was over, we flowed into the night wind with an exiting audience so deeply affected that nobody spoke above a whisper. Slowly, we made our way through the echoing streets back to Taaffes.

"Shall we go back in?" Liam asked, in one indecisive moment before the unmarked door. He held open the door when I nodded, and we entered into the parallel universe of Taaffes.

"Liam," a voice wafted from somewhere in the crowd. Like a domino effect, people moved in a whirlpool until a tall young man with dark hair and eyes clapped Liam on the back and said, "How you been keeping?"

"This is Tomas," Liam said to me, emphasizing the second syllable. "This is Hailey." Tomas shook my hand.

It was so noisy in Taaffes that I wondered if I'd heard his name correctly. "Tomas?" I asked. "Is that right?

"Yah, bit unusual name but not so unusual for these parts," he said, holding two fingers up, catching the bar tenders eye. "Here, take this seat." He pulled a stool out from the bar for me and he and Liam stood on either side. "It's an old name from the time of the Spanish influx in this area, actually."

"Well I like it. Is The Spanish Arch on Galway Bay

from the Spanish influx?" I asked. "Was it Spain that built the arch?"

Tomas laughed. "That's a common misunderstanding. The arch has nothing to do with the Spaniards, it was simply built as an extension of the walls that protect the quays," Tomas said. "They started building the arch in the early part of 1580 and didn't finish until well after the threat of invasion was over."

"Anything happening in Ireland tends to happen slowly," Liam added.

"I've heard about you, Hailey," Tomas said, when Liam was out of earshot, talking to someone just a couple of feet away.

"Good things, I hope," I said.

"Well, I heard about Liam looking for an American girl around town the other night. No doubt the girl was you." He put his elbows on the bar and leaned in conspiratorially.

"Apparently, you and everybody else in Galway heard that."

"Well, I've been to America; we're a much smaller world here. Very few of us can do much undetected," he said with a subtle smile.

It's funny how things can turn on a dime. It's not that I haven't always known they could, it's just that I don't walk around expecting it, so when they do—and I'm talking about bad news—I'm always caught off guard. All I can do is stand aside baffled, looking in hindsight at what has transpired. I've always thought it's a shame that when conditions are in the process of turning irrevocably, we rarely see it coming. It would be so convenient if we could. Then, when things turn on a dime, if nothing else, we could at least save face.

Pulling into my driveway, Liam turned off the engine and sat looking at me for an extended moment. "Will I come in?" he asked.

"Of course," I said.

I found my keys and unlocked the living-room door. Switching on the lights, I saw Liam settle himself onto one of the high stools beneath the kitchen counter. Taking off my coat, I walked around the counter to stand beside him. He reached out his arms and pulled me in close between his bent knees. My arms over his shoulders, I placed my hand on his hair and leaned the side of his face comfortably beside my own. We kissed passionately and stayed in this position for what seemed a delirious eternity. Time suspended itself as I felt his hands slide beneath the back of my sweater. Slowly, I took a half step back, and his hands caressingly crept to the front for the first time.

"Do you want to stay?" I asked, completely unplanned. This time, I was ready.

In less than an instant, both hands were abruptly gone. I steadied myself, registering the moment, as if cold water had just been splashed on my face. I saw him place his hands on his knees at the same time I took a step back, trying to get a better look at him. With the clearance I had given him, he stood up and walked purposefully to the other side of the kitchen. He sat down on the kitchen floor with his back against the wall and hugged his knees in tightly before him, lowering his chin in what looked like a closed-off, fetal position. I looked down at him, thinking his body language was telling.

"What is it?" I said, when I had found my breath. He shook his head discernibly.

"Liam?" I searched.

"It's not you, it's me," he said after a moment.

I let the words resound for a second, trying them on for size. "What about you?"

"I have something I need to sort out on my own," he said. He looked down at the linoleum floor, withdrawn and sulking over something mystifyingly unnamed.

After a long pause, I said, "Does this have something to do with somebody else?"

He shook his head quickly. "I don't understand myself," Liam said.

"You'll work it out," I said slowly, the fear in me beginning to rise. After a few beats, I added, "Or maybe you won't."

He nodded, continuing to avoid my gaze by staring blankly at the floor.

"I'm just confused," he confessed.

I was baffled. I hadn't seen this coming, and I couldn't imagine why he was so confused. I thought about trying to draw it out of him by sitting down beside him, perhaps encouraging him to articulate what it was he wanted to say; it was apparent he wasn't going to volunteer anything without me doing something along that line. Then I started thinking if I did, it was only going to turn into a question and answer forum that felt like pulling teeth. I decided not to play. He was injuring my pride enough as it was. If Liam had something to say, he was going to have to say it on his own. Neither of us said anything for what felt like an eternity. I thought Liam waited for me to prod him into confession, while I waited for him to simply volunteer.

"Liam, to tell you the truth, I'm confused too," I finally said.

"I bet you're confused because I'm confused," he said softly.

"Well, there's definitely that." I paused. "Let's just

say your confusion tells me a lot."

"I'm not saying what you think I'm saying," he said, sounding hurt.

"All I'm thinking is you're not saying very much of anything, Liam. If you have something to say, then for God's sake, say it."

"I just have something I need to sort out," he said again, which seemed to me like a retrograde movement.

"I'll tell you what," I said, the fear in me continuing to grow. "I think you've said all you need to say for now. I think two people have to mutually agree to stay in the game. It should be easy, you know? If you're hesitating, if you have something you need to sort out, then go ahead and do it. Let's just leave it like this: if you ever figure it out, then get back to me." I folded my arms across my chest and looked down at him. I was irritated, hurt, and defensive.

Liam's eyes darted to me, then back to the floor, they grew wide for a second, then closed tightly as he loudly sighed. He stood up and looked at me intensely, although he still didn't speak. He drew in a breath, then exhaled audibly. He walked slowly to the door, hesitated, turned to me and said, "I feel like something bad has just happened here, and I caused it."

"It's all right," I said, looking at him with dagger eyes. I couldn't help it, I felt rejected.

He placed his hand on the doorknob, then quickly yanked it opened as if he couldn't walk through it quickly enough. I heard the porch door close heavily and then he was gone.

I remained where I was until I could no longer hear the leaving sounds of his car on the driveway, and then I found the nerve to move. I walked out onto the porch, shutting off the light so I could look out into the night without obstruction. The stars hung thickly in the sky over the sea, and the night was suddenly windless. I reached for the handle on the glass door thinking Liam probably just touched this for the last time. I pulled the door open and walked outside without a plan. Looking up, I wanted the stars to reach down and embrace me because I wanted to find a way for this sinking feeling to disappear. I pulled out a cigarette to self-medicate, and lit it with shaking hands.

Making my way to the wall in front of the house, I sat down, inhaling way too deeply. *These are the things we do when we're trying to fill the void,* I thought. *Wonder what I should do once this cigarette goes out?* I sat with my legs dangling down the stone wall, replaying the scene in my mind. *If I were anybody else,* I thought, *I would have tried to baby Liam, tell him that it was all right, and that I'd just sit around demurely and wait until he was sure about me. If I were anybody else, I would have tried to talk him into being less confused about me. That's what a lot of women would have done.*

I wondered what he was thinking at the moment—if he was even thinking about it at all. I wondered if he had planned to have things go the way they did or if we, in our inexperience, had irretrievably mishandled ourselves. Perhaps what had really happened was that Liam was afraid, I had been defensive, and we were both so wrapped up in our own self-absorbed fear that we were unqualified to meet the requirements of the moment by simply communicating. I sat on the wall turning it over until I realized the only real question was where do I go from here?

Bad news has a way of traveling whether we like it or not. I don't recall having made a decision to tell anybody other than Shannon what had happened between Liam and me, but within the next couple of days, it seemed everyone I knew had something to say about it. I was superstitious about that. I kept thinking talking about it negatively would keep it locked up in a negative place, and if I kept thinking of it negatively, then it would never have the chance to turn around. I told myself of course it had to turn around; it was just a question of time. It was bound to have been a misunderstanding. Sooner or later, Liam would see that clearly and come around. Thinking this way, however, did not make the wait any easier.

I had just finished telling Shannon the edited details when Declan burst through the door of the Centre. He stood looking from one of us to the other then back again.

"Who died?" he said enthusiastically.

"Prince Charming has disappeared," Shannon answered.

"Are we depressed?" He looked at me anxiously.

"Yes, we're depressed," I said flatly.

"What happened?" he volleyed back.

"He's confused." I met his eyes.

"Mama's boy," he said with derision, and then he turned abruptly and trudged demonstratively upstairs to get his guitar. Thundering back down, Declan seated himself before Shannon and me and began singing the song, "Feelings" in his unintelligible Derry accent. He kept it up all day, singing one depressing love song after another in between the coming and going of the day's business, and he was absolutely priceless. Under any other circumstances, I would have been tickled into hysterics, but as it was, I just recognized it as Declan's unusual way of commiserating with me. Although there was an element of humor to his antics, Declan conducted himself in a more subdued manner that day, asking very little of me, and every now and then looking at me with penetrating eyes asking, "Are we still depressed?"

At two o'clock, Declan said, "Let's knock off for a while. We're all too depressed over Prince Charming."

"Knock off and do what?" Shannon asked.

"Let me take youse to lunch. We'll go to Le Graal. I think we should go on the piss."

"Great idea," Shannon agreed.

"All right, that ought to solve everything," I said gloomily.

Declan picked up a pen and notebook and quickly wrote something down. "We don't have to solve everything," he turned to me, opening the door and locking it behind us, "we just have to solve this today."

"Declan's rules for Alcoholics Anonymous in reverse," Shannon said.

When the three of us walked outside, Declan pushed the paper through a nail on the door. I turned around to look. In large uneven print, the note read:

"Two o'clock. We're on the piss."

Chapter Fourteen

It was misting heavily outside as I walked from New Road toward Henry Street. Everywhere I looked, I saw the color gray: the street, the sidewalk, the buildings, and the sky above. I knocked on Deanna Rader's door and was ushered inside by her younger sister. The fire inside roared, and beside it sat Deanna's mother and father with a pot of tea on the table before them. Even though it was late afternoon, the room was dark, there being no opportunity for light to come through the two, small windows of the living room. I took off my coat and sat down beside Mrs. Rader.

"Dreadful weather," she said by way of hello. "All the way with us from Letterfrack, so it was."

"Time of year." Her husband nodded in agreement.

"Hailey is in for her first Irish winter," Deanna said, handing me a mug for the tea.

"I understand you've had the pleasure of meeting himself?" Mrs. Rader gestured toward her husband.

"I have," I said. "Nice to meet you as well."

"You're from America, are you?"

"Memphis, Tennessee," I answered.

"Ah, yah, Elvis and all the rest," she said, nodding. "Are you long here?"

"Yes," I said, thinking there's that question again.

"Oh, that's grand." She smiled, looking at me without blinking. "You don't have a pick on ya, do you?"

"I guess not," I said.

"Lovely hair you have, God bless it."

"Thank you."

"Must have taken ages to grow that."

"Actually, I don't recall ever having it much shorter than this," I said wanting to get the focus off me. "Did you just come down from Letterfrack?"

"We did, yah. Just came down to do a little shopping," she said.

"There's nothing in Letterfrack," Deanna volunteered.

"Don't be talking that way about the land that raised you," Mr. Rader reprimanded.

"Well, it's true," Deanna said, "you have to come into Galway to get anything done."

"Must be nice there," I said, "I've never been to Letterfrack."

"It's peaceful. God's country," Mrs. Rader said. "Not much opportunity for the young ones to run the streets."

"So, I moved here." Deanna gave me a wink.

"Speaking of running the streets," Deanna's sister said, "time is wasting."

"All right then. Enough of us sitting around with the tea." Mrs. Radar got up and reached for her coat. "We're away, so." When the three had left, Deanna and I moved in closer to the fire.

"So tell me," she said "any word from Liam?"

"Of course not," I said sarcastically. "That would imply he actually got it together and came over to see me."

Deanna looked thoughtful. "He's afraid, Hailey."

"Maybe," I said. "Who knows?"

"We should go and see Harriet today," she said. "She'll know."

"The card reader?" I asked.

"Yes. We should walk up to Eyre Square and call out to her."

"Right now?"

"Oh, yah, she'll be there, all right."

"Don't you have to make an appointment?"

Deanna looked at me as if I were speaking a foreign language. "For what?" she asked.

We walked up Henry Street, turned left on Dominick Street, crossed O'Brien's Bridge and continued up Shop Street until we reached the back entrance into Eyre Square. Pulling the heavy, wooden double doors open, we stepped into the midst of what looked like a crowded, indoor flea market. Tables of every height and size stood cluttered together, covered with odds and ends for sale while vendors from all walks of life stood selling their wares behind them.

"Harriet's in here," Deanna said, pointing to a four-post, curtained partition with a standing sign that read: "Readings: 12 euros." I picked up a clipboard with a sign-in sheet and saw that Harriet was free at the moment. Deanna leaned her head through the slit in the curtain and I heard her say, "I've brought a friend."

I parted the curtains and pulled out a chair across from Harriet, who sat at a table ceremoniously covered with a green-and-gold silk cloth. She was an astonishing, ageless looking woman with an unlined, full-moon face crowned with short, ivory hair that hovered above a black, turtleneck adorned with a silver Celtic cross hanging halfway down its front. Her blue eyes were the color of clear innocence; they shone brightly like circular aquamarine. Not a sketch of makeup did she wear, yet when I looked at her face, the color pink radiated seemingly from the core of her being and emanated outward like a halo. She handed me an oversize card deck, which she instructed me to repeatedly shuffle. When I awkwardly wielded the big cards in both hands, three cards fell loosely from the deck. I began to retrieve them immediately, but Harriet abruptly stopped me.

"Wait." She scooped the cards up and examined them closely. "When a few jump out like this, there's a message coming through." She lowered her eyes and studied them. "The Empress, the Fool, and the Chariot," she said, handing them back for me to fold into the deck. "Continue," she said gravely. "Put your energy into the cards." I continued, alternating between mixing and shuffling. "Take your left hand and cut them," Harriet said, as I followed her lead. Picking up the deck, she laid the cards out one by one, in a pattern she seemed well versed at placing.

"Is there a young man giving you trouble?" she immediately asked.

"Yes," I said.

"He'll come back," she said. "You're a lot alike. There is a lot to talk about between you two."

I looked at the cards as if I could see what she saw. The Emperor was the first card, under it was The Devil and beside it was The Lovers. I saw the Strength card in the spread, yet couldn't make out the others, so unfamiliar was I with the deck. She picked up a card and said,

"Someone is giving him bad advice, maybe a mother or a sister. Someone is creating mischief; stirring things up; giving him bad counsel. He's going to discard it and carry forward. He is in love," she said. "He'll be back. By December," she said after a pause. "Did somebody die?" she said looking at me closely. I froze.

"Not too long ago," I answered.

"Was he a musician? Did he leave any songs behind? You should look at getting them published," she said. "Do you now feel liberated?"

"Not really," I said. "I think this is another story."

"He's around you." Moving on she said, "Give me

170

your hand." She paused as she turned my palm over, scrutinizing its lines.

"Tell me about your dreams."

"Sometimes they come true," I said.

"You have two mystic crosses in your hand. You may count on your dreams, and you can trust your intuition. I see your name lit up in lights. Tell me your name so that I can remember you. I see fame headed your way. By the way," she said, "you're terrible with finances."

I smiled. She was right.

"Right now, you're not sure what you're doing. I see an Atlantic crossing soon, a reunion. Is he going with you?" she asked.

"No plans," I said.

Harriet took a short, deep breath, looking at the spread before her. "I see a time lapse before you, a wait; you must have had a very serious relationship before; this next time you will use your head and it will last forever," she said. "This will come after your Atlantic crossing. Don't be impatient for the young man who's giving you trouble. He's never been in love before," she concluded. I smiled at Harriet and handed her twelve euros plus a tip. "Thank you," I said.

I walked out from behind the curtain and looked around for Deanna. She stood laughing loudly with a woman she appeared to know, who was selling some sort of something from a table in the back of Eyre Square. I walked over, and Deanna quickly turned. "What did she say?"

"She said he'll be back. Sounds like he's going to take his sweet time."

"She's brilliant, Harriet, isn't she?"

"I'm not sure what to think," I said. "Uncanny

though, some of the things she said."

"If she says he'll be back, he'll be back," Deanna said with certainty.

Realizing the time, I said good-bye to Deanna and walked the half block to Eyre Station to take the last bus back to Inverin. The mist that had been with us all day had now heightened to a heavy rain. I climbed onto the bus, angling my way down the aisle. Out of the corner of my eye, I caught six young men in the back of the bus, blatantly watching me. I made no eye contact, but could literally feel the movement of energy around them. Sitting down, one of them sidled up and maneuvered into the vacant seat beside me. *This is all I need,* I thought. I looked straight ahead, minding my own business, but he started in anyway.

His name was Bill Reilly, and he wanted my full story. He said he was from Inverin, but now lived in Manchester, England, where he was working in construction. I decided I was in it now, and finally looked over the shoulder he rubbed against, making eye contact. He was a big, brawny, good-looking young man who looked to be in his mid-twenties. With medium-length, brown hair he wore under a baseball cap, his face was broad and handsome, defined by a masculine, straight nose and dark blue eyes. He presumptuously started talking to me about male and female relationships, as if he had already won my confidence.

"What would you do if you gave everything you had, all of your love to someone and they rejected you?" Bill Reilly asked. "What if you did that, and they threw it all back in your face?"

"I don't know," I said, thinking the subject was ironic coming from a complete stranger. "Sounds like you've been there before," I said.

"I'll tell you what it does: it makes you never want to do it again!" he exclaimed.

Is this guy the opposite of Liam or what? I thought.

"Where in Inverin do you live?" he wanted to know.

"Across the street from the Centra," I returned.

"Oh, yah. Do you know many people there?"

"Not in Inverin as much as I do in Galway."

"Do you know the Hennesseys?" he asked, out of the blue.

I couldn't believe it. *What are the odds,* I thought. I suppressed a sigh. "Yes, a little," I said.

"Which one?" he continued.

"Liam."

"I used to play football with Liam, but I know Anthony better. We're the same age. I'm going to be seeing Anthony tomorrow, as a matter of fact."

"Is that right?"

"Listen, next time you see them, tell them you met Bill Reilly."

"Why?" I asked.

"Just tell them you met me, and watch their face," he said with a devious smile.

"Why should I do that?"

"Just watch them," he winked. "I've a bit of a reputation."

"Okay. I'll mention it."

"I'm going into the Cruiscan when we get to Spiddal," he said. "Come have a coffee with me."

"I can't," I said automatically.

"Oh, yes you can," he said with a laugh.

"All right. For a little while," I conceded. I was thinking: *What would that hurt? What will I be doing, upsetting Liam?*

I walked into the Cruiscan with Bill Reilly and made

immediate eye contact with Tomas, who got an eyeful of Bill and me walking in, and immediately turned away. *This is going to be nationwide,* I said to myself.

Bill ordered two coffees at the bar while the bartender described the minutiae of some soccer match he'd recently seen, walking back and forth animatedly behind the bar. After about twenty minutes, I started thinking it was time to go. I got up, thanking Bill for the coffee.

"I'd like to see you again before I go back to Manchester," he said. "Maybe I could call out tonight, or tomorrow night; we could catch some music here or at Hughes or something."

"Not tonight, maybe tomorrow," I deflected, in that way you do when you've already decided that's never going to happen.

"All right, I'll call out tomorrow around seven or something," Bill Reilly said.

"You can't go!" Shannon said the next day at the Centre. "You'll run into Liam! You've got to find that guy and tell him you can't go!"

"You're so right," I agreed.

"That will ruin everything; Inverin is too small. You'll run into Liam, or his brother, or his father; it'll ruin everything."

"I'm not going, Shannon, I just conveniently won't be there."

"All right. Good. We have to talk about Declan."

"What about Declan?"

"He's disenchanted again; he told me last night."

"Where was this?"

"In Taylor's."

"I miss everything living out in Inverin," I said.

"I think he's serious; he doesn't want to man the fort of a rehearsal studio. Now he's saying that's not what we're there for; we're supposed to be helping Irish musicians with their careers only, and he's impatient about the time it's going to take to get funding and all of that. I personally think he's running out of the money Owen gave him. I think he's paying out of his own pocket."

"How much did Owen give Declan, anyway?" I really wanted to know.

"I think about thirty-thousand euros," Shannon said. "I think Declan's been living on that as well."

"But the rehearsal room is bringing money in," I pointed out.

"Obviously not enough."

"Aren't Declan and I supposed to go see Silas Burke this Saturday?" I recalled.

"Yes, you're supposed to; but now he says he's not going. He says it'll be a waste of time."

"I'm fascinated by how capricious Declan can be," I said. "It's something different with him every week. Where is he now?"

"I don't know. He hasn't come in yet."

"What time is it?"

Shannon looked at her watch. "Just past noon. Look, I think Declan is losing his motivation for the Centre and since you and I will be going home for Christmas in a little more than a month, he just doesn't see how he can keep the Centre operating by himself."

"Where's Adrian!" I looked at the ceiling and rolled my eyes.

"Really. You know, Darren has found part time work at Monroe's," Shannon said. "He's tending bar."

"So, he won't be around either. I don't know,

Shannon; I have to go home for Christmas. My mother will kill me if I don't. She already thinks I've absconded to another country."

"Mine too," she said. "I've also got to fly to Los Angeles and meet with my advisor at UCLA. I'll be gone for two months."

"Let's just wait until Declan shows up," I concluded. "We can talk to him then."

Declan never appeared at the Centre that day and eventually, I went back to Inverin and nervously watched the clock as it crept toward seven. I had settled upon telling Bill Reilly that I was sick. Lame excuse that it was, I figured there was no arguing it. I paced around nervously as the seven o'clock hour came and went. It was eight o'clock when I started thinking I'd been stood up, and by eight thirty, I was glad for it. I went back to my bedroom and started changing out of my clothes. From the distance, I heard a car door slam. I stood still as the beat of my heart grew louder. I looked at the clock and saw it read a quarter till nine.

Remaining where I was, I decided I was totally justified in not answering the door because Bill Reilly was close to two hours late. I glanced out of the bedroom door and was grateful to notice that I had not turned on the lights in the living room. *Lucky break,* I thought, as I heard the rap on the door. Again and again it came, with persistence building upon urgency. After ten minutes, it finally stopped and I remained in my bedroom, keeping a low profile for the rest of the night.

Chapter Fifteen

It was an unusually mild Saturday morning for the end of October wherein the wind was uncharacteristically subdued. I fumbled with a tin of Bewley's Irish coffee and the new French press I'd bought and hoped the day wouldn't prove to be an exercise in futility.

"This ought to be good," I had said to Shannon after two days of a no-show from Declan. "Two Americans going to see the Irish Minister of the Arts, asking for a business grant in Ireland."

I walked to the phone booth in front of the Centra and called Mick Folan before the bus into Galway came round the hill. When he answered the phone, I said I'd like to come around later this afternoon and bring my guitar.

"Finally," Mick said. "I'll be expecting you in time for tea."

I walked to Shannon's flat on Nun's Island Road around ten thirty. Mrs. Donoghue came to the door wearing an embroidered apron, drying her hands with its hem. "Yes?" She looked at me suspiciously.

"Mrs. Donoghue, I'm Hailey, I've come to see Shannon," I said.

"Shannon, is it?" she responded, not moving out of the doorway.

"Could you please tell her I'm here?"

"Does Shannon know you're coming to see her?" she interrogated.

"She does. We have plans today."

Mrs. Donoghue closed the door and left me standing on the sidewalk. I walked out to the street, looked up at Shannon's bedroom window, put my index fingers together and whistled sharply. Shannon's head appeared through her window's lace curtains. "Will you call off the guard?" I called up.

"Just a minute." Shannon disappeared, and a moment later, she opened the front door.

"What's wrong with that woman?" I stepped inside. "Maybe you ought to give her your daily itinerary or something. What's she think I'm going to do? You'd think there was a threat of kidnap." We climbed up the stairs to Shannon's room.

"Any word from Declan?" I sat down on her bed.

"No, nothing. Any word from Liam?" she looked at me, concerned.

"No. He's probably with Declan. In fine old Irish tradition, they've both just disappeared."

"That's about the size of it." Shannon picked up her purse. "The Irish don't do conflict. You ready?"

"Yah, let's go," I said.

Jury's Hotel sticks out like a sore thumb down by the quays of the river Corrib in Galway and is absolutely incongruous to most everything around it. It is a modern hotel in a town painstakingly dedicated to historic preservation. Immediately surrounding Jury's Hotel are the Spanish Arch, the Historical Museum of Galway, and McDonough's Fish Market, which all stand prominently on the cobblestone streets. "They should have thought this one through," I whispered to Shannon as we walked through Jury's modern lobby. Shannon went to the front desk and asked the man behind the counter where we could find Silas Burke.

"He's in the room there at the moment." He pointed toward the back of the lobby. We entered the room and Shannon approached a woman seated behind a small desk.

"Do we need to sign in?" Shannon asked the neatly dressed receptionist.

"No, just wait your turn," the woman said, not looking up.

Shannon crossed the room and sat down beside me. "We're supposed to wait our turn."

"I heard. Of course, it occurs to me nobody else is sitting here waiting," I said.

"I knew you were going to say that." Shannon shot me a sideways glance.

With no discernible prompting, the woman at the desk eventually glided over, clasped her hands together, and dutifully announced with a tip of her head, "He'll see you now." Shannon feigned gushing enthusiasm. "It's our turn!" she said with animation.

"Stop making me laugh." I elbowed her in the side as we walked to the bay window where Silas Burke sat behind a wood panel partition.

The first thing I noticed about Silas Burke was he bore an uncanny resemblance to the author Samuel Clemens—or Mark Twain as he's best known. He had glowing white hair that stuck out every which way, and untamed eyebrows that matched. A coarse mustache swept hither and yon to either side of his mouth as if it were fighting gravity. He'd assembled himself into a blue pin-striped shirt beneath a gold-buttoned, navy blazer with an unnecessarily loud red tie.

I kept thinking for whatever reason, he'd woken up this morning and decided to pattern himself in an outfit the colors of the American flag. Quite the theatrical man, Silas Burke was attentive, gregarious and verbose. He gestured wildly with his hands to the point of distraction while he spoke, but I was not deflected. Nothing he could have done would have camouflaged the fact that he spoke in confusing doublespeak. He gave all pretense of taking us seriously, yet in the end, he promised nothing. He vaguely implied our case would be "considered" for a grant from The Irish Arts Council, and closed the meeting with the proclamation, "Youse at The Galway Music Centre will be notified when your time is due."

The second we walked out of Jury's Hotel, Shannon turned to me and said, "What just happened?"

"We just met the master of the art of placating," I said. "Allow me to translate this time; I'm getting better at Irish-speak. 'Our case will be considered' means on the off chance a bolt of lightning hits me in the head and shakes the thought of your case into my mind, I might bring myself to think about it, and 'You'll be notified when your time is due' means we're standing at the end of a very long line and will probably be taking this one to our graves."

"At least we followed through with going to see him. What are you going to do now? Want to come with me to see Darren?" We started walking toward Eyre Square.

"Thanks, but I'm going to go back to Inverin to see Mick Folan."

"All right, try not to let anything else happen out there, will you?"

"Really," I said, "it's rarely a normal scene anymore."

"Hopefully Declan will materialize Monday."

"This is weird," I said. "I can't believe he's doing this; he's acting like a little kid."

"Declan's just inexperienced," Shannon said. "His entire identity is tied up in the Centre because it was his vision first, you know? He told me once he was going to give it a year; we're pretty close to that now. I think Declan's afraid of failing. He doesn't want people to say I told you so. I think he's worried about money because he's mishandled what Owen gave him. He expected us to receive funding by now. I think he's worried about losing control of things as well. You know how he can be."

"It's uncanny the way you can read him. What bothers me is that we're all friends so it feels like a breach of friendship. He's being completely disloyal."

"Yah," Shannon agreed, "kind of dishonest, too. We'll see where he's coming from when we talk to him."

"I forget sometimes you're in all of this because of school," I said, as we veered toward the bus station.

"That's how it started. I mean, that's what got me over here, but now the Centre has actually turned into something. We're definitely filling a need here in Galway, and I think we're being recognized more than we realize. The potential exists to become a successful business or nonprofit organization, but I have a feeling leading it takes more responsibility than Declan is willing to shoulder," Shannon said. "My motivation is all about writing my thesis, but it's also to finish what we started. Things are just starting to happen for all of us. Darren and I both think Declan just needs to take a vacation. It'll be okay."

"Yah, one way or the other," I said with a sigh.

The front door was wide open when I arrived at Mick and Gabrielle's house in Inverin. The walk through the bog had taken me longer than usual because I'd been carrying a D-series, acoustic guitar. I walked in and set the guitar case down on the threshold. I called Mick's name and waited for a response from somewhere within the house.

"I'm in here," Mick's voice echoed from somewhere down the hall.

I followed the sound of his voice to the dimly lit kitchen. Mick sat before the fireplace in an old rocking chair looking freshly shaved and expectant. He held his guitar on his lap and, setting it down, said, "I've been singing me heart out all day in preparation for your arrival." He extended his arms. "Let's have a look, then." Delicately, I handed over my guitar. Mick set it on the floor and unbuckled the latches. Lifting the guitar out, he placed it on his knees and began to strum slowly, feeling each string tenderly as if he were caressing fine silk.

"Ah, she's a fine spirit." He looked at me intently. "Nice action; Martin guitar, indeed."

I sat Indian-style on the hand-woven rug. He handed the guitar to me, then picked up his own, stopping suddenly. "Now, before we get started, I'd like to offer you some advice."

"All right." I balanced the guitar and waited.

"You know the stream that runs through the bog there?"

"I do." I nodded.

"I suggest you take your guitar down there for a wee listen to the stream. Just sit and have a chat with her. Ask her where her sound comes from. This is important. Listen and then listen some more. You'll be able to hear her. Her voice will be inside your soul. I know you know how to connect because you're a Celt. All you need do is put yourself aside and feel. Ask her where her sound comes from and where it's going. When you and the stream understand each other, when you've connected hearts, then leave knowing that the sound of your own heart also has a source, just like hers. I mean to tell you, you and she have the same source. Music comes from that source. It's all one thing happening." He stood up and walked to the kitchen table. "So, your first lesson is to listen."

"Okay." I watched him retrieve a pen and yellow legal-sized notepad, then walk back to the rocking chair where he drew a careful graph of guitar frets, placing dots on the lines where my fingers should be.

"Here, look closely at the drawings. This one is an E chord." He looked into my eyes with a look that tore right through me while he strummed an E chord on his guitar. *If looks alone could teach me to play, then by the end of the day, I'd be a master,* I thought. From the E chord, Mick took me through the chords of D and A. "Now put them all together, like this," he said, strumming a rhythm that shaped itself into a melody. I strummed along, looking down at my fingers as I tentatively placed them on the strings. "It's Van Morrison's 'Gloria,'" Mick said, smiling like a magician who'd just performed a feat of magic. I smiled back, recognizing the song and trying to find the ease of the rhythm.

"Hello, Hailey." Gabrielle entered the kitchen with Solas by the hand. "How's the lesson?" Snapping out of my focus, I shook my head.

"I don't know what to say. It feels like a foreign language right now."

"She's grand," Mick said with a wave of his hand. "She'll be up and running in no time."

"I probably have to get used to the size of the guitar first," I said. "It's hard to get my arms around it."

"She's a bit big for you, I'll give you that," Mick said. "You'd be better suited with a double O from looking at the size of you. You're only a wee slip of a girl, you."

"It's not too big, though. I can still learn on this, can't I?"

"Oh, God, yah, of course you can," Mick said. "Let's

leave it here for now, let you work with what you have. We'll go from there."

"Okay, thanks a lot, Mick, seriously. I'll always remember my first guitar lesson came from you." I stood up slowly and went to the window. "I guess I better get going, it's getting dark."

"Are you walking home?" Gabrielle asked. "If you want, we can give you a lift, but if you're going to walk then I'd like to walk with you. I could use the exercise."

"Okay, let's walk," I said.

Mick buckled my guitar in its case. I gave him a quick hug while Gabrielle shrugged into her coat. We set out on the gravel road that led back into the bog, crossed the bridge over the stream and started the incline that traveled between a lone house and an open pasture with scattered sheep.

"Do you have any idea why some of the sheep have pink paint on their coats?" I began.

"I think they belong to different herders," she said, drawing out the word herders in her fluid French accent.

"Do you ever walk this part of the bog?" I asked. "It's the prettiest part, you're lucky to live so close by."

"I never thought of walking for pleasure. Mick and I thought you quite strange when we would see you out here on your own. In France, I would never walk for pleasure. We thought it must be an American thing."

"I wouldn't say it's an American thing as much as I'd say I've always loved taking long walks. You can see a lot more if you travel on foot; it just gives you a better feel of your surroundings."

"Right," she agreed.

"The first time I saw you and Mick together, you were out here walking around, weren't you?"

"Yes, but we were probably just getting out of the

house to avoid a fight."

"Do you two fight a lot?" I asked, thinking they probably did.

"Mick and I are learning how to live with each other," she answered thoughtfully.

"How long have you known each other?"

"About three years now. We met in France. We fell in love, but then Mick came back to Ireland. He was running away from love."

"Running away from love? Why?" I wondered if I was being given all the facts.

"Because he's Irish. Irish men are afraid to love."

"Is that how you see it?"

"That's how they are. You must know that if you've ever loved an Irish man," Gabrielle said.

I considered Liam's weird behavior, and all I felt was unresolved. I didn't know if I should keep it to myself, or say something as long as we were having the conversation.

"I've never heard anyone say that before. I haven't known a lot of Irish men, only casually dated someone, if you could even call it that," I said.

"Mick tells me you see someone who lives here in Inverin," she said.

"Does everybody know everything about everyone around here?"

"Yes," Gabrielle said. "Everybody knows everything about Mick and me, and I don't know half the people that do."

I paid close attention to what Gabrielle was saying. The conversation was evolving from small talk to important information.

"How did you come to live in Ireland?" I asked.

"When Mick finally returned to France to see me, I

told him we were in love and should be together. When he returned to Ireland, I came with him. It was a struggle until I became pregnant with Solas. Even though he loved me, Mick was afraid of being tied down."

"Maybe it's not all Irish men that are afraid to love, maybe it's just Mick," I suggested.

"I think it's the men here. How is it with your friend?"

"My friend has disappeared."

"Disappeared, ah," she exclaimed emphatically. She didn't seem surprised in the least. In that one moment, I stopped taking Liam's actions personally. In that one moment, I was just talking things through with a friend, examining evidence as if it were a case study that had nothing to do with me, which was a huge change in perspective.

"Tell me about him," Gabrielle said.

"Everything was fine, or at least I thought it was until he told me he was confused," I said.

"Was he your lover?" she asked pointedly.

"No," I said.

"You see there? He is afraid," she concluded.

"Afraid of what?"

"Irish men are afraid of being in love because they lose control. The women in this country trap them with babies at an early age, and then it is all over for them. They think it is better not to love. They think there is no risk if they push the love away." When delivered in a heavy French accent with her vehement attitude, I was thinking Gabrielle had a valid argument.

"But I wasn't trying to trap him," I said. "I pretty much told him the exact opposite."

"What did you tell him?"

"I told him to go on if he was so confused," I said.

"Now he must be really confused. Perhaps other women have clung onto him in the past and you did not. If you told him to leave, then he has no real reason to run," she said. "He won't know what to do now."

"I can't figure out why he has to do anything. Everything should be a lot easier than this."

"Love is never easy, especially when the man is afraid," Gabrielle said.

Chapter Sixteen

Shannon and I spent the following week holding down the fort at the Centre with no word at all from Declan. On one of those days, Bernard O'Malley walked through the door looking for Declan. As it turned out, Declan had neglected to pay October's rent, and all Bernard wanted to know was what in the world was happening.

"We haven't heard from Declan either," I told him. Bernard stood taking the information in with both hands on his hips, looking down at me with his intelligent blue eyes.

"From the looks of things, I'd say the rehearsal room is doing well, yah?" he queried.

"Amazingly so," I confirmed.

"So, it's not all bad, then, is it?"

"Not completely."

"If it turns to trouble, I want youse to come to me," Bernard said decisively.

"I will. I'll let you know everything I know, all right?"

"Right, have Declan call out when you see him. Good luck, all the best," Bernard said, walking away.

It wasn't until the following Monday that we finally received a phone call from Declan. I stood on the stairs to the loft while Shannon talked to him. Hanging up the phone, she shrugged with an audible sigh. "He wants us to meet him at Café du Journal tomorrow at four o'clock."

"In other words, the operating hours of the Centre no longer matter; we'll just close down early and go, right? Not a good sign," I said. "By the way, what's so pressing in his life that he can't meet us today?"

"Who knows? All we can do is wait until tomorrow. He owes me a wage for the last three weeks. What about you?"

"Same for me," I said. "I don't know about you, but I'm having a hell of a good time being in a foreign country illegally without an income."

"Let's just hope this will be short-lived," Shannon said.

Café du Journal on Quay Street is an artsy little coffee shop in Galway. An extremely small place, it has local art on the walls and diminutive tables crammed together from corner to corner. Chairs are randomly scattered throughout the aisles, so it's the patrons' responsibility to create a seating arrangement. Shannon and I arrived at four and found a table. It was ten minutes to five when I said, "Do you think he's coming?"

"Yes, I think he's coming," she said. "He probably just wants to keep us in suspense and come in here making a grand entrance."

"I bet you're right. He tends to do everything with huge dramatic flair, doesn't he?"

"Everything without exception."

"He rarely gets a rise out of you, but Declan drives me crazy because he's so erratic. He's topping himself this time. I can't help but notice his flagrant irresponsibility, I'm kind of taking it personally," I said.

"Believe me, you shouldn't take anything he does personally. Declan doesn't have a malicious bone in his body."

"I know, you're right. It's just that he operates in such a self-centered vacuum that the people around him get caught in the vortex, know what I mean?"

"Oh, I know," Shannon said.

"If you think about it this time, it's entirely different," I continued. "He owes you money; he owes me money; he owes Bernard money, and he has conveniently chosen to disregard it all by not addressing it. Do you remember the last time Owen came to the Centre unannounced, and Declan slithered outside with him then came back in not bothering to share anything with us?"

"Slithered out like a snake," she added.

"Like a guilty snake," I said.

"Yah, I remember that." Shannon nodded.

"I had a feeling then that something was up."

"That was his sin of omission," she said.

"Look, it's not like I'm keeping score, but the past couple of months have been weird. Declan hasn't been acting right. He's been confrontational over little things. Maybe it's me," I said.

"It's not you, Hailey," Shannon said quickly. "It's just that you're doing something very specific by helping to organize musicians' careers. A lot of them can't do that for themselves, and Declan didn't envision a kind of artist representation thing happening at the Centre."

"It created itself, in a way," I said. "I don't know. Declan has been there all along. He could have stopped anything he didn't like at any time; he could have said something."

"Well, on the one hand, he wanted the Centre to evolve into something, and on the other, he wanted to be the one who came up with all the ideas so that you and I and Darren could execute them. It was all supposed to be his idea."

"So, what you're saying is it's all about him," I said.

"The Centre always has been all about him—in his mind anyway."

"So, am I to blame for trying to get anything done?" I asked. "What do you think?"

"Not any more than I am, or anybody else," she answered.

Just then, a dark head of hair appeared out of the corner of my eye and came toward the table. It was Declan, and he had cut off his ponytail leaving a one-inch buzz cut all the way around his head. He wore Levi's, a white T-shirt, and a blue madras shirt hanging unbuttoned. Pulling up a chair, he squeezed in close. I looked at him without saying a word.

"Nice haircut," Shannon said in that deadpan way of hers.

"It suits me, doesn't it?" Declan patted his head.

"Why did you cut off your ponytail?" was all I could think to say.

"I needed a change," Declan stated.

"Does that go along with any other changes you intend to make?" I asked.

"Jumping to the point, Hailey?" He raised his eyebrows.

"I thought I would. Don't forget Americans are direct. I'd love to wait around indefinitely to figure out what you're doing, but I don't have the time," I said.

"All right, I'm sorry," he said on an exhale. "I know I should have called out to youse. I've been busy."

"Busy doing what?" Shannon asked. "You haven't been busy at the Centre with us."

"Why don't we just get down to it," I said. "Declan, you called and asked us here. Was there a reason for that?"

"Yes, I want to close the Centre," he said. Shannon and I exchanged looks.

"Declan," Shannon began slowly, "it's too soon to

close the Centre. It hasn't been a full year yet, and there are a few things in the works you're probably overlooking."

"I'm not overlooking anything," he shot back.

"Yes, you are," Shannon volleyed. "For one thing, it's taken us all this time to get the word out that we actually exist. Now that people in town are aware of what we're doing, we're starting to get a few interested sponsors asking questions. I'm not certain anything will come from the Arts Council—I don't think you know Hailey and I went to see Silas Burke—but maybe we'll get funding from them. In other words, we haven't seen that possibility through yet."

"And, the rehearsal room," I added. "Declan what's your problem? Just tell us. We can help you sort it out."

"I just think I'm putting all this work into the place and getting nothing back. There are so many expenses, and we haven't had any funding all along. Owen was thinking we were going to be this grand investment. It's just a load of things."

"I thought it was to be a philanthropic ideal anyway," I said. "I've never been clear about Owen's role in the scheme of things. I mean, I'm not sure what sort of agreement the two of you have."

"I can take care of Owen," Declan said defensively.

"Did you run out of money?" Shannon cut to the chase.

"I don't think that's your concern," he said quickly, as if it were a prepared statement. Shannon and I exchanged glances again.

"The books are in Roscrea," Declan said. "I know I owe youse two money. I have to go down there and get the books first."

"What are the books doing in Roscrea?" I asked.

"I left them at a friend's house last weekend. I needed to get away," he said. I looked over at Shannon, who rolled her eyes.

"What, you don't believe me?" he whined.

"And the dog ate your homework," I said. "Declan, for God's sake."

"Well obviously we need to be paid," Shannon said. "Other than that, can we leave it at this? Don't do anything yet. Let's keep the Centre open and wait until closer to Christmas, then we can see where we are."

"You'll be leaving in less than two weeks to go back to the States," Declan said. "And then Hailey leaves after that, then what? Am I supposed to do everything by myself?"

"I'm not gone yet, Declan," Shannon said. "Hailey has another month or so."

"All right. Let me think about it. I'll call out to the Centre and chat with youse tomorrow," he said, concluding things.

We separated on the street outside Café du Journal. Declan left in a hurry, claiming he had somewhere he needed to be.

"Dramatic enough for you?" I said, watching Declan speed away.

"Really," she said. "Let's just see what happens tomorrow."

"All right. I'm going over to Mill Street to catch the bus out of here. I've had enough for one day."

The next day, I woke up earlier than usual with the nagging feeling something was going to happen. I paced around, looked at the clock, and decided to take a walk outside before the day began. I headed out my front door toward the main road and took a right turn up the street

193

instead of turning left into the bog. As I walked, thinking about all of the immediate variables in my current situation that were not appearing to come together, I saw the early bus into Galway rising over the hill from Carraroe. *Maybe all of these things are adding up to some sort of a bigger plan, and everything just appears to be in disjointed bits and pieces because I don't have the big picture,* I thought.

When the early bus into Galway drew near, I looked at the driver and waved. I continued walking onward, deep in thought until it hit me. *When did I become one of those people who waves at the bus driver?* I thought. For a brief moment, I forgot everything that weighed me down and laughed out loud. The morning was cool and I was thinking, *whatever the day is going to bring, I'm up for the challenge; all I have to do is get an aerial view.*

By nine twenty, I was stationed at the bus stop, then rode into Galway, dismounting at the Spanish Arch. Walking toward Quay Street, I decided to take a route to the Centre I'd never taken before. I recalled Liam telling me about the Corn Street Mall in Galway, and thought maybe I'd go find it. He had said it was as upscale of a place as you'd ever find in town, and that he bought imported red wine from a store in the cluster of the Corn Street shops.

I walked through the entrance of the outdoor mall and found the wine store he referred to. Standing close to the store's front window, I looked in briefly, then followed the sidewalk as it wound its way between stores on either side of the lane. Coming to the last window, I noticed a contemporary-styled café, so I glanced through the window out of curiosity. Straight before me, at a table three rows removed from the glass, Liam slouched over a book with a coffee mug before him. I located the door of the café and, without forethought, walked straight into the restaurant, over to the table where Liam was sitting, and sat in the chair across from him.

"Hello, Liam," I said. He looked up, eyes wide.

"I knew I was going to see you today," he said, although the size of his eyes told me he was shocked.

"They say most people born under the sign of Cancer are fundamentally psychic. That's you, isn't it? Weren't you born in July?" I asked. "Or do I sound like I've spent way too much time in California?"

"Not at all," Liam said. "My psychic abilities are a convenient tool of mine."

"Lucky for you," I said. It was then that I realized how nervous I was. My thoughts were racing, looking for hidden meaning.

"So, how have you been?" he asked.

"Fine," I said.

If he knew the confusion he's added to my peace of mind in general, he wouldn't be asking me how I've have been, I thought.

"And you?" I returned.

"Ah, just grand," he said. "Busy."

Too busy to recall you ever met me? I wondered.

"Oh yah?" I was surprised at how neutral my voice sounded. "Busy doing what?"

"I'm making a recording, actually, and I've started teaching children to play the accordion. I'm giving lessons."

What? You're making a record and teaching kids? What cosmic avalanche happened to reroute your life? I felt like saying.

"That's great," I said. "They're lucky to have you."

God, I'm going through the motions of this, I thought. *What was the name of that movie where the hero and heroine met after a period of estrangement?* I wondered. *They were so nonchalant when they reconvened.* I wondered how in the world they did that.

"Well, I'm starting out small," Liam continued, "there are just a few students at the moment, but I'll see how much time I have for it. How's the Centre?"

"Not very good. Declan is saying he wants to close it, maybe before Christmas. Words can't describe how erratic he's been. He's been putting Shannon and me through hell."

"Ah well, a tiger showing his stripes, I imagine."

He never did like hearing about Declan, I recalled.

"Something like that," I said.

"What will you do if Declan closes the Centre?" he asked.

"I'm not sure. I haven't thought that far ahead." The following moment of silence made me uneasy.

Wait a minute, I thought. *Liam hasn't taken the initiative to see me; this is just a chance encounter. This doesn't count. What am I doing sitting here chatting?*

"Well, I guess I better get going." I stood up.

"Would you like a cup of coffee?" Liam suddenly asked.

"No thank you," I responded automatically.

"Do you mind if I get another?" I shook my head and sat back down.

I guess I'm supposed to sit here and wait, I decided. *I've been trying to read this guy's sign language from the moment I met him.*

"I've been meaning to return your poetry to you, but I've been putting it on the long finger," Liam said when he returned.

"Liam, exactly what does the long finger mean?" I asked.

Liam laughed. "You know, I've been putting it off for another day."

Because you don't give a damn, I interpreted.

"I see, interesting expression," I said.

"So, I'll bring the poetry out one of these nights."

He's being awfully vague, I observed.

"All right," I said.

"I can leave them on the porch table if you'd like," he offered. I nodded.

Oh, I can just picture that, I thought. *He'd leave my poetry on the table and run. I'm already exhausted with second-guessing him. This one's up to him.*

"Or, we can go out for a drink if you'd like." He didn't meet my eyes.

He's testing the waters for my response, I concluded. *Maybe I should help him out.*

"I'd like that, Liam," I said. "I'll see you any time. I think you and I really get along. I'd be happy to see you any time."

There now. I didn't mince words; there's nothing ambiguous here. Probably just hit him over the head with my Americanism, but that's okay, I told myself.

"I know we get along," he said softly.

Then why'd you disappear? I wanted to ask. *All right, this is getting awkward*, I decided

"I really should be going," I said. "Shannon will be at the Centre by herself, more than likely."

"What time will you be leaving today?" Liam stood up with me.

"Probably around five."

"Can I give you a ride back to Inverin? I'll be in town up until then as well."

What is this, coincidence? I wondered. *Is he just saying this?*

"That would be great," I said.

"What time shall we meet and where?" he asked.

"How about five at the Lisheen?"

"I'll be there at five," Liam said.

At five o'clock on the dot, Liam walked through the front door of the Lisheen carrying a plastic bag from Kenny's Bookstore. I had arrived ten minutes before him, and was sitting on one of the dark wooden benches that lined the front wall.

"Will we move to a table?" He stood over me. "Would you like a drink?"

"Sure," I said. "If you have the time. What's in the bag?"

"Poetry from Patrick Kavanaugh."

"Will you read some of it for me?" I asked when we found a table in the back room.

"I'm Irish," Liam said. "We don't do that." I looked up and noticed he was blushing. He must have forgotten he'd read Patrick Kavanaugh to me before, but I decided to leave it alone.

"How was your day?" he sat down.

"Declan didn't bother to come in today, even though he said he would. No surprise there."

"Ah, then," Liam said.

I got the impression a long time ago that Liam was not really interested in the Centre. His mind didn't work that way. The things that interested him were outside of the realm of business, so if ever he did inquire about the Centre, I kept my answers short because I knew he was only being conversational. A waitress appeared, and Liam ordered two pints of Guinness.

"Do you think I need a haircut?" He ran his hand through his hair. I looked at him, realizing his hair had grown a few inches. Because it was so dark and straight it had a dramatic affect that changed his look from conservative to bohemian. I wondered if he'd intentionally decided to change the look of himself. If he had, I wondered what had brought that on. For some reason, I was unsettled by the change. I was thinking it communicated he was doing just fine without me in his life, that he was making self-improvements in his forward progress. Then I decided I was blowing it out of proportion, making a big deal out of nothing.

"Your hair is longer than I've ever seen it. I think it looks nice. It makes you look more like Heathcliff," I said.

"Then I'll keep it," he said.

It's funny how time and distance can give you clear thinking. Sitting there in the Lisheen, it was as though I was looking at Liam in an entirely different light. Maybe it was because the fire had been extinguished, and the smoke had cleared. I noticed little things as I sat across the table. For one thing, he was capable of being a nervous wreck. I'd always considered Liam to be the epitome of self-possession, but as I watched him, I saw how extremely self-conscious he was. For another, he spoke abstractly, choosing to speak generally as opposed to specifically, and it made me think he was speaking in veiled messages.

"I've found myself getting tangled up lately over past issues," he said out of the blue.

"What do you mean?"

"I don't know. I mean, I don't know why I do that."

"Past issues?" I encouraged.

"Yes," he said. "Most people dwell on the past, or long for the future when the best thing to do is live in the present," he said. "I know that, yet I get tangled up anyhow replaying things in my mind when I should be paying attention to the present."

Is he alluding to us? I immediately thought.

"Maybe that means there's something bothering you that needs rectification," I said. "It's normal to think about a scene or conversation you've been involved in if you're trying to make sense of it. Maybe you need to readdress or correct something."

What I wanted to say was, "*Liam, if this is about the last time we met, then what is it you're trying to say? Are you sorry you acted the way you did? Did you say something you didn't mean? Has it made you so confused you couldn't get it together to come back and address it?*"

I wanted to ask, but had been in Ireland long enough to know that would be socially unacceptable. From my American vantage point, there seemed to be a subtle dance the Irish employ around any charged topic even when they're trying to say something specific. It's as if the higher the stakes, the vaguer they become.

Liam looked down at the table with his eyebrows drawn together. I thought about Shannon saying to me once that the boy must be in pain. I decided it was for the best to make things easy on him.

"Liam, you're a smart guy," I said. "I think everybody mulls things over, and it doesn't necessarily mean they're not living in the present. People don't have a choice but to always live in the present, the way I see it. If the present means you're looking at what happened in the past, it doesn't mean you're not still in the present. Don't get all tangled up thinking you're not thinking correctly in the moment. That just creates more self-conflict."

"That's typical you." He smiled broadly.

"I'm just trying to make sure you don't create your own hell." I smiled back.

We left the Lisheen at five thirty and began the ride to Inverin. We were both a little uneasy, but primarily I felt we were trying to reconnect. Glancing at the road ahead, Liam observed the pending rain. "You can feel it'll be any minute now," he said.

"All right," I said, "we've descended to an all-time low. Is it my imagination, or are we talking about the weather?" I asked.

Laughing at me, Liam said, "It's an Irish cultural hazard."

"Okay, fine; I'll add it to the list, but I'm telling you, way too many things in Ireland are a cultural hazard," I said.

"I've got another one for you: I'll be meeting a friend of mine at the handball court by your house soon," he said. "The last time I played, I couldn't play my instrument for two weeks. Anyway, I'm to meet him at six fifteen."

Pulling in my driveway, Liam looked up the road. "I see his car there, I guess I'm late." I put my hand quickly on the seat belt release, not wanting to detain him.

"Thank you so much, Liam," I said. "It was great to see you."

"I'll call out for you one of these nights and we can go for a drink," he said immediately.

"I'd like that," I said. "Anytime."

Afterward, I felt good about it, and then I felt relieved, but later on that night, I worked it up to a point where I wasn't so sure. Technically, nothing had been resolved; we had only faced each other. I found it interesting that fate had provided the chance encounter. It seemed to me that if we, in our human frailty, didn't have the courage to take care of business, then the powers that be intervened seemingly by chance.

Chapter Seventeen

Although I had little reason to go into Galway, habit held hard, so I gathered my things and walked down the road to the bus stop. It was Monday morning and the Friday before, Shannon and I had simply locked the Centre door three hours after we got there and gone on home. Since Declan had not shown his face that day as he said he would, Shannon and I had little recourse. We parted company without trying to guess what the next step would be.

I unlocked the door of the Centre and walked up the stairs. On the computer in the loft was a note from Declan: "Hailey, call me on my mobile Monday at six p.m.," it read. I retraced my steps and walked to Shannon's flat on Nuns Island Road. This time, she answered the knock on the door.

"Declan has a mobile phone." I walked through the front door.

"He's moving up in the world," Shannon said. We went up the stairs to Shannon's room.

"It doesn't sound like he'll grace us with his presence today," I told her. "He wants me to call him tonight at six."

"So what do you want to do today? Should we go in?" Shannon sounded doubtful.

"Were you planning to?" I asked.

"Eventually. I have to get ready to go home, though. I think we should just keep the doors open like we planned until I go. We might as well."

"That's what I've been thinking. Anyway, we did tell Declan that was the plan. Even though he's still being flighty, we should do it with or without him."

"We need to tell Bernard what's going on," Shannon said.

"I'll do it. Tell you what, why don't you just get there when you get there today, and I'll see you whenever."

"Okay," Shannon said.

On my way back to the Centre, I stopped at the front door of Bernard's house and rang the doorbell. Bernard's five-year-old son opened the door wearing dark blue overalls and a matching knit hat. "Is your da home?" I asked. The child looked up for a second, turned abruptly, and ran with a clatter down the worn wood floor of the hallway. A moment later, Bernard walked toward me holding his son by the hand.

"Come inside, now, will you have a cup of tea?" Bernard said in that lightning-quick way the Irish have of running all their words together. I followed Bernard back into the kitchen and stood leaning against the counter while he put on the kettle.

"I've come to tell you what's going on," I began.

"I know all too well what's going on," Bernard said. "Declan is in hiding. I called out to his house on Knocknacara Road and he's moved."

"When was this?" I was caught completely unaware.

"Friday, midday. Darren's brother has been living there. He told me Declan moved out last week."

"Did he say where he went?" I asked.

"Hadn't a clue," he said.

I looked at Bernard, not knowing what to say. The entire picture ran through my head. It was Declan's responsibility to pay Bernard rent at the first of each month; if he wasn't doing that, then that was going to be it for all of us.

"I'm sorry about this, Bernard. It looks like you know

what's going on, though."

"Oh, I know what's going on and no surprise to me. Your man's been talking in circles these last few months anyway," he said, audibly drawing in his breath.

"Shannon leaves in a little more than a week, and I'll be going in the middle of December," I said. "We've been talking about just continuing until then, but if Declan isn't in the picture, then it kind of changes things."

"Listen, it's not your fault. I've been doing some thinking on me own," Bernard said. "I've seen the people come and go here and I'd like to keep it happening. I see the rehearsal business is steady. I've been thinking about adding on another room and just having it be a rehearsal business."

"That's not a bad idea," I said.

"I might be able to work on the second room over the holidays, by January it could all be ready," he said.

I was thinking Bernard had the right to do whatever he wanted with what we started on his property. As I stood there in his kitchen, I waited for him to just say it: the decision had been made, he'd be taking over and making the changes.

"Well, hopefully Declan will show up and pay you what he owes," I said. "He still hasn't paid Shannon or me for the last couple of weeks, and we're waiting on that as well. Sooner or later this will all be cleared up."

"To be sure," he said. "Listen I'd like to chat to ya about staying on here. I'll be needing someone to stay with the rooms and run the place. I'm not the one who knows the young folks playing music, don'tcha know."

"True," I said enthusiastically.

"We can sort it out later," he said. "I'll have to look at it and chat to you about a wage. I'm not sure what I can offer yet; let me see if I can sort it out."

"Okay," I said, relieved. "I'll let you know what happens next. I'm supposed to call Declan tonight."

I left thanking my lucky stars for Bernard O'Malley. Walking back to The Centre, I looked toward the door and saw Adrian standing before it. "How's the form?" he said by way of a greeting.

"The form's been better, Adrian," I said, putting my key in the door.

"I've brought you my poetry, like you asked," he said.

"Great, Adrian, come on in." I opened the door and flipped on the lights in the front room.

"Do you want some tea? I've noticed it cures everything in Ireland."

"What are you looking to cure?"

"You haven't by any chance seen Declan lately, have you?" I crossed to the kettle.

"As a matter-of-fact, I have indeed," he said. "He's moved in with your man on New Castle Road."

"What man is that?" I turned, looking at him.

"One of the musicians from the Wakefields," he said. "Remember me playing you their CD a while back?"

"Of course," I said. "Their ex-drummer is now playing with Leigh McDonough. What's his name? Aiden?"

"Aiden Dunlop," Adrian said, "but it's not him, it's another guy from the band."

"So where on New Castle Road is this?" I was curious.

"Well, I wouldn't be wanting to tell you exactly, but I could point you the way," he said.

"All right, be evasive. I'll let you point me the way just the same, and no one will be the wiser. First let me have a look at what you've brought."

I'd already rehearsed how to respond to Adrian's poetry. I knew he'd be watching me closely while I read, and I wanted my response to be flattering. He handed me a three-ringed notebook, full front to end.

"Is there any place you want me to start? I know it's hard to show people your stuff for the first time."

"Anywhere is fine," Adrian said.

"What did you write last?" I asked. "I know with me, my favorite poem of all times is the last one I wrote."

"Don't be ridiculous," he said.

"Why? Aren't you that way?"

"Not at all; it'll all do."

"Okay, fine," I said.

I opened his notebook to a random page and started reading some of the most sophisticated and fully realized poems I'd ever seen. With a delicate hand, Adrian wrote of time, nature, and rural settings in beautiful metaphors that hinted at the search for a place in the world.

"This is really good, Adrian," I finally said, as if it were the first time I had ever truly seen him.

"It is, yah?" The humility in his voice was touching.

"Seriously, Adrian," I returned, glad to really mean it. "Thank you for showing me this."

"Well, I said I would," he said. "I like to be a man of my word. By the way, how's Prince Charming?" he asked.

"You wouldn't believe it if I told you." I set his notebook aside.

"I would," he said. "Tell me."

"All right." I took a breath and quickly outlined Liam's disappearance and our subsequent chance encounter. "That's the abbreviated version; I haven't a clue what to make of it. I only know I'm tired of trying to figure it out. It seems he's afraid or something, I don't know."

"I wouldn't worry about it too much, Hailey," Adrian said sensitively. "You can't take it personally. He's a traditional musician, you know. What you have to understand is those trad guys are married to the music. The music will always come first. His father is a musician, yah?"

"Yah," I answered.

"Well, you have to look at how Liam was raised, probably by his mother, who now has a big influence on him. The da was more than likely always off in the pubs playing most nights, and I'll tell you, none of the musicians around here live much differently. Liam's living that life right now. There's no time for a woman."

"Then why did he start coming around in the first place?"

"No doubt, he doesn't know himself. He just did, and it sounds like he started thinking about it afterward. Then he ran."

"I have a friend from France who thinks Irish men are afraid to love," I offered.

"Oh, no, we're great lovers, all right. We're just afraid of being tied down too early," Adrian said. "Have you ever noticed how many really young mothers are around Galway? Don't you notice those young girls pushing prams around?"

"I guess so," I considered.

"Even though this is the twenty-first century, we're still a bit shy on birth control. We've been so long thinking it was a sin, you know. Love around here means sex; sex means babies; babies mean marriage, and it's all the one thing." He tried to make me understand.

"I hear you, Adrian, but Liam knows I'm not trying to do that. I've told him as much."

"So, he's heard the words," he said, "that doesn't mean he believes them."

As I listened to Adrian, I was thinking how wrong Declan was about him and how often it is that people judge others at face value. It may have been partially true; Adrian was a little lost, a little adrift in life, but he had a wealth of insight and more sincere compassion than anybody I could think of in that moment.

"All right," I said. "Thanks, Adrian, thanks a lot. I know you don't want to be involved in any more Declan drama for the rest of your life, but if you're willing to show me where he lives, I promise I won't ask anything further from you. It's important that I keep on top of him, though."

"All right, let's walk." Adrian picked up his notebook and rose from his chair. Eventually, we found ourselves before a low, wrought-iron gate that heralded the walkway of a two-story, redbrick house on New Castle Road. "Now, I'm only pointing the way," Adrian said.

"I know," I said. "You're not culpable. I'm supposed to call Declan tonight. This is just in case something funny happens and I need to locate him in the future."

"Right," said Adrian, and winking at me conspiratorially, he turned and walked away.

At six o'clock, I walked down to the phone booth in front of the Centra in Inverin. I put my calling card in the slot and dialed Declan's number. After what seemed like incessant ringing, he finally answered the phone.

"Yah," he said.

"Declan, it's Hailey," I said. "You wanted me to call you."

"Oh, Hailey," he said. "Yah, I'd like to chat to ya. Can you meet me tomorrow?"

"Yes, I can meet you tomorrow," I said trying to hide

my exasperation. "Where?"

"Café du Journal at two o' clock," he said, sounding serious.

"I'll be there tomorrow at two," I said.

The next day, I was at Café du Journal at two o'clock, and Declan was not.

I don't know what it is that takes you over the edge to the point where you've definitely had enough, but the next morning, I took the early bus into Galway and, although I hadn't planned it, walked straight to New Castle Road. It was ominously dark outside and the rain pouring down in thick black curtains shut out the sun entirely. Pushing through the creaking gate, I knocked on the door beyond a reasonable time for it to be answered. If I had to stand there all day, I was prepared to do it. Eventually, a skinny, young man clad only in a bath towel opened the door. "Is Declan here?" I asked curtly. "Upstairs." He moved out of my way.

It was as dark inside as it was out, and I had to peer into two mistaken bedrooms before I finally found Declan. The room was small and rectangular with a window in the back and not a scrap of furniture except for the narrow twin bed pushed against the wall. I walked lightly on the wooden floor and stood looking down at the bed to make sure it was Declan who was in it. "Declan," I said sharply. Startled by the surprise of my voice, he sprang bolt upright in bed, covering his torso with a thin white blanket.

"I was going to call out to you today," he said quickly.

"Of course you were," I said.

"I was," he repeated.

"You're cornered." I sat down on the bed beside him.

"I'm mad at you and Bernard," he began.

"Are you, now," I said with forced patience, "do tell."

"I talked to Bernard yesterday, and he told me he wouldn't give me back the deposit for the Centre unless you were standing there as a witness."

"I love it." I laughed. *Good old Bernard,* I thought.

"That's low," he said in a disapproving tone.

"Declan, under the circumstances, you've got a lot of nerve," I observed.

"Why are you discussing me with Bernard?" he accused.

"What, do you think you're operating in a vacuum? You've created a web around you, you're shirking responsibility, and you think you're not affecting anybody? What is the purpose of scheduling meetings or saying you're going to do something if you have no intention of following through?" I said all at once.

"Look, I know I owe you wages, but I don't have it," he confessed.

"All right, now we're getting somewhere," I said. "This is the first time you've leveled with me. Does Owen know?"

"Yes, Owen knows, and he's on the warpath against me."

"Well, there it is." I let out a deep sigh. "No point in playing cat and mouse anymore, is there?"

"I'll get you your money before you leave. Shannon, too," he said.

"That's between you and Shannon, but I hope you don't string her along much longer. The thing is, Declan, one either has a code of honor or one does not. You might want to think about that. You can do the right thing or not; it's up to you." I knew I had reached the end of the conversation with Declan so I stood up to leave.

"What are you going to do?" he asked.

"Why, at this late date, would that concern you?" I walked out of the room and closed the door behind me.

Chapter Eighteen

I sat on the porch, looking out at the night sky while I weighed my options. The way I saw it, things could not be more uncertain: Shannon would be leaving soon; Declan had bailed out of the Centre and out of my life as far as I was concerned; Liam had been keeping his distance; I had no income, and Bernard was taking his time deciding what he could offer. I knew I needed to get a plan quickly. It felt as though I was at the whim of too many capricious people, and it was making me feel powerless. I needed to make some decisions about what to do next; I needed to take control. It wouldn't be long before I, too, would be returning to the United States for Christmas.

It crossed my mind that I should stay once I got there, but then I asked myself what I would do if I stayed. I thought about how it would be working for Bernard. Probably great, I concluded, but what about the rest of it? The circumstances I had come to know in Galway had unraveled, and the people around me had dissipated. I got up to get my journal. On the steps before the living room, I noticed an envelope marked airmail. I picked it up and walked inside. Setting the envelope down on the kitchen counter, I looked at the post date on the letter's right corner. The date was three days prior, and I thought that couldn't be.

Opening the letter, I saw my former employer in Los Angeles' signature. The handwritten date at the letter's top was the same as the post date. *This is weird; it always takes at least ten days for a letter to reach Ireland from the United States*, I recalled. An offer to return to my old job was before me. It seemed the woman who had hired me at the record company would be leaving to have a baby, and the offer to replace her was being given to me by the managing director. I set the letter down and pondered the date of it one more time. *What in the world is this?* I thought, *Cosmic intervention?*

The managing director wanted me to call him as soon as possible so we could talk further. *It wouldn't hurt to call,* I told myself. As much as I didn't want to live in Los Angeles, it couldn't hurt to explore the offer. Maybe it would only have to be for a little while; maybe I could give it one year and return to Galway with a little bit of money in my pocket. *The timing of this is uncanny,* I thought.

I called the managing director from the phone booth outside the Centra, and stood looking out toward the sheep and grazing cattle in the fields that led to the sea. Absorbing his succinct American accent and the authoritative presentation of his offer, I thought he sounded like the voice of reality floating in from the outside world. The wind howled to a fevered pitch against the phone booth while I visualized him in his office, all clean-shaven and suited up. I realized I was a long way from home. *He's in the real world,* I thought. *What am I doing in a phone booth in Inverin?* "Let me think about this for a little while," I said. "Can I call you back in two days?"

The managing director asked me to forward him a business plan outlining exactly how I'd improve the department, and I stood there thinking, *He doesn't have a clue how unrealistic this request is. I'm so far removed from how the real world operates that I can't fathom a plan.* I told him I would, then told myself I'd follow Liam's example and put it on the long finger. I had much to think about. I was being offered a serious position in a serious business. *There is certainty here,* I thought. *If I play my cards right, I can return to Galway within the year or so. This would be amazingly responsible of me; it would be the logical thing to do, and I don't exactly have another choice.* Two days later, I called the managing director and accepted the offer. I hung up the phone and, since I was standing in the phone booth, picked it back up and called Liam Hennessey without hesitation.

"Hello?" Liam's mother answered the telephone.

"Hello, I'm calling for Liam," I said bravely. *Typical,* I thought, *I knew this would happen.*

"Liam, yah? Just a minute there," she said. A moment later, Liam's father came on the line.

This is getting worse, I thought. *Did I predict this, or what?*

"Oh, I'm sorry, I meant to ask for Liam Og," I said— Og meaning Jr. in the Irish language.

All right, I thought, now everybody knows who's calling. No big deal, I'm leaving soon, no big deal.

"Hello?" Liam came on the line.

"Hi, Liam," I said. "It's Hailey."

"Ah, Hailey, great to hear from you," he said cheerily.

"Listen, the reason I'm calling is to tell you that I'll be leaving Ireland in four days. I'd like to see you before I go," I said.

"And then you'll be back after Christmas, yah?"

"Well, actually, no," I said. "I'll be staying in America for a while; I've got a job there."

Liam paused and then said, "Would you like to meet tomorrow night?"

"Tomorrow would be fine," I said.

"Early then? I'll be in Spiddal until five o'clock," he

said. "I can call out afterward."

I thought quickly. "Why don't we meet at the Spiddal Pier," I suggested. "I'm going to say good-bye to Seamus Kearney at the end of the day. He lives next door to the church on that road."

"The Spiddal Pier it is, then," he said, "at five."

I hung up the telephone and walked up the hill to my house with a surprising feeling of relief. It had been so easy to just pick up the phone and call Liam. *Maybe I should have done that a while ago,* I thought, but then again, I'd never had a concrete excuse to do it.

The reason I was going to say good-bye to Seamus Kearney, the dapper old man I had encountered on the bus into Galway, was because I had crossed paths with him the day before. As I stood at the post-office counter in Spiddal thinking about Seamus living right across the road, in one of those strange, coincidental moments, I looked to my right and there he was standing shoulder to shoulder with me like an apparition.

"I was just thinking about you," I said, stifled by my inability to articulate just how weird it was to see him standing there.

"And to what do I owe this honor?" Seamus bowed.

"I'm mailing a few things back to the United States," I said. "I'll be leaving in a few days. I have a job there. I'll be calling Los Angeles tomorrow to accept it," I had told him.

"Leaving, is it? You'll be leaving us for how long? When will you be coming home again?" he inquired. I liked the way he implied that Ireland was my home, and in that moment I felt torn and indecisive.

"I'm not really sure when I'll be back," I said. "I'm thinking about getting some money together, and then returning in about a year. It looks like the Galway Music

Centre will fold, and it just seems like the right thing to do."

Seamus looked at me, registering the information. "Well then, why don't you come over to the house for tea the day after tomorrow; you can give an old man a proper good-bye."

"I will," I said automatically. "Really, the day after tomorrow would be perfect."

"How does four o'clock suit you?" he asked.

"Very well," I said. "I'll be there."

Of all the things I would miss about Ireland, I would miss the long walks I had grown accustomed to the most, which is why I decided to walk to Seamus Kearney's house all the way from Inverin. I wanted to walk the coast road into Spiddal one last time, and I did so heavy with longing and nostalgia. I knew that in a few days' time, I'd feel the burden of separation and displacement. I walked past the open fields and intermittent houses I'd seen so many times before, missing everything already. I was now familiar with the terrain and every facet of the road; I knew what to expect around every bend, and as I walked, I looked around sealing the images in my mind, thinking that soon, all this will be only a memory. I acknowledged that there was a tug-of-war going on within me, setting my emotions and my powers of reason at odds beyond reconciliation.

Leaving Ireland was the practical thing to do, but I wasn't completely ready to do it. I had not exhausted my appreciation for the land, the warmth and character of its people, or the way I compatibly fit in. It felt to me that something was being interrupted and I began to worry that maybe it was the story of my life.

Surely, I thought, *this is the right move to make and*

I'm reading the signs correctly. The events of late were obviously connected; they couldn't have been meaningless. All roads for me were leading out of Ireland for some reason, and I had to have faith that fate was not conspiring against me. What I wanted more than anything else in the world was to not misinterpret the signs. It occurred to me that perhaps there was something waiting for me on the other side. It was either something or someone, I decided. "In Los Angeles?" I said aloud with disbelief, knowing there was no one near to hear me talking to myself.

Why is it, I thought, *that when you need it most, a voice doesn't rain down from above telling you what to do, so that you don't mess up your entire life.* I considered the fact that if I were to hear a voice from above, then it wouldn't matter what it said because it would probably mean I was crazy. *This must be an age-old desire,* I said to myself: *To have the answers shouted to us from without, when the only answer worth listening to comes from within.* I knew better than to think otherwise. I was reading the signs, wasn't I? All things were pointing the way back to the United States, weren't they? I finally decided I'd be doing very well to keep the faith and just follow. I was in it now, and there was no getting out of it.

I pulled myself together and knocked loudly on Seamus Kearney's door. He opened it immediately with a smile that lit up the doorway. He looked absolutely splendid in his dark gray suit, white shirt, and striped tie. The lengths he had gone to in preparation for my visit tugged at my heart, for here was this gentle, old man who had carefully spread a tablecloth in the living room and put out a beautiful display of brown bread, Irish butter, strawberry jam, scones, and an apple pie enough to feed a large group. As my eyes swept the room, I stood there thinking if I really let in the depth of kindness in this gesture, somebody would have to help me off my knees. Plates, napkins, and silverware were arranged around cups and saucers and a blue ceramic teapot. Seamus had thought of everything, so I enthusiastically helped myself with exaggerated gusto since he'd gone to all the trouble.

We sat balancing our plates and facing each other on matching straight-back chairs in front of the welcoming fire.

"So, it's leaving us you are, is it?" He looked at me with gravity.

"The day after tomorrow. It happened quickly, and at a curiously opportune time in a lot of ways."

"That's usually the way of things." He smiled wistfully. "Will you miss it here?"

"Yes, definitely. I feel I was just starting to know my way around. I'm used to everything now. Things that seemed foreign to me when I first came here now seem to be just as they should be. It's fascinating moving to a new country. At first you measure everything according to what you know but after a while, the ways of the new place replace everything, if that makes any sense."

"It does, yah." Seamus nodded. "Eventually you become part of the fabric. We're a queer folk, the lot of us, but once you come to know these parts, you realize there's no harm in our ways."

"I think people here are a lot different than Americans," I said. "I could tell immediately just from the way people speak. It's primarily the phrasing: people here enter their conversations kind of sideways, talking in circles around a topic as if it were rude to actually get to the point. It's a specific way of communicating that leaves a lot to the imagination of outsiders."

"Well, Ireland is an old culture," he explained, "and

old cultures are subtle cultures. We're like most of Europe that way. There is a great respect for language that I don't think you have in America. We're colorful in our language, all right. You know, I was a language teacher at the boy's school across the road for many years."

"I don't think you told me that; what language did you teach?"

"English and Irish both. You have to keep in mind that the way the Irish speak English comes loosely from the translation of Irish words into English words. In Irish, there are more relationships positioned between things. The English language is more direct, in other words, it has less connections holding it together. When I say connections, I'll give you an example: in English, you would say 'It's a nice day.' To say the same in Irish it would come out as 'It's a nice day that's in it.' You see? In Irish there are more relationships between words and that means more possibilities, as well as more room for uncertainty. Therefore, even though there are more opportunities for uncertainty, the possibilities in communication are endless, it just depends on where your mind is." He winked at me. "That may be why you perceive us as jumping around the point whenever you hear English in these parts. A few things are twisted in the translation but to me, it's a better way of being human."

I had to take a minute with that. "I'm glad to hear your explanation," I finally said. "I think it's more than that, though. I'm trying to think of how to articulate it. It's as if there's an unspoken understanding that coming out and saying what you really mean is not an option. It's like it would be bad manners or something."

"Oh, I see now." Seamus looked at me knowingly. "It's love, is it?"

I could feel my face turning a flushed red. "I don't

know if it's love, I mean, if it was love," I clarified.

"Oh, it's was, is it? And you can't be sure because it wasn't discussed enough to make you sure," he concluded.

"Something like that."

"Young lad confusing you, is it?" he asked. I nodded while he nodded along with me. He drew in his breath audibly, the way the Irish do when they're getting ready to say something poignant.

"When I first met my wife, who is no longer with us; God bless her and a fine one she, I didn't have the words to tell her anything, no, nothing at all," he shook his head with a nostalgic smile. "We're not one for spilling the soul around here, and you'd be best not looking for it," he said.

I thought about Seamus having a wife. Of course, he had to have had one. In looking around the living room, I saw pictures of children individually framed, and one of a young man in uniform. There were others scattered across the room on various tabletops and shelves, but from where I sat, I couldn't make them out clearly.

"How long were you married?" I asked Seamus.

"Thirty-eight years. I have three wonderful sons by her, and five grandchildren. It was the cancer that took her in the end."

I'm always so sorry to hear things like that, and I always wonder what it is I can say beyond the rote words of, "I'm sorry." There's not enough covered in those two words, and too many people use them perfunctorily. "She was lucky to have you," I said. "And your sons, are they living here in Ireland?"

"They all are." I could hear the pride in his voice. "All married and on their own, they are, and a large part of my life."

"Good," I said, and I meant it.

"Back to your young lad," Seamus returned. "Do I know him?"

"Yes," I said, thinking there's no harm in saying it now. "Liam Hennessey, but don't say anything to anyone."

"I'm the soul of discretion." Seamus put his hand to his heart. "And he wouldn't talk to you, was it?"

"It's not that he wouldn't talk; it's more like he disappeared out of nowhere," I said. "He came around for a long time, and then all of the sudden, he stopped. I accidently ran into him recently, and we both acted as if it hadn't happened, I mean, we never really addressed it. He said he wanted to get together again, which makes it even stranger. That's why I was saying it seems to me people around here keep things to themselves."

Seamus looked deep in thought. "That's odd." He shook his head. "Then you wouldn't want him, would you? Once something like that happens it's never the same anyway."

I was grateful that Seamus had stated the obvious, and more so that he thought it was odd because it immediately confirmed my feelings. Whether Liam's behavior was a cultural thing or not, it was odd by Seamus's standards, and that was enough for me. "I'll be seeing him today at five," I told Seamus.

"Then you leave the day after tomorrow," he added.

"Yes."

"Ah, that's odd," he repeated, shaking his head again.

I rounded the driveway beside Seamus's house and began to walk down the road that leads to the Spiddal Pier. Although I had been watching the clock on his mantelpiece, at five minutes until five, Seamus had stood

222

up and said to me, "The time is nigh."

"Thank you, Seamus," I had said.

"Godspeed to you, then," he said. "Return to us safely."

I walked toward the pier thinking this time I was going to let Liam do the talking. I was conscious of the way I was walking, as if I had all the time in the world, when of course I didn't. It was one of those sauntering walks that belie the fact that you're a nervous wreck inside and I just wanted to get it all over with because I felt like a death-row inmate taking the final tour. I didn't see Liam's car anywhere in sight, and I entertained the possibility that he had chickened out.

I climbed the wall of the Spiddal Pier and sat on the ledge facing the road. I recalled the night we had unexpectedly stumbled upon Patrick and Evie, and then it dawned on me this was the exact spot where Liam and I had gone on the first night we met. I was thinking about full circles and the karmic adage of what comes around, goes around when I saw Liam's car drawing near. I reached in my coat pocket and pulled out my little camera. The picture I took of Liam as he walked from his car to my side is the only one I took of him the entire time I was in Ireland. When our eyes met, he noticed the camera and drew his arm up to cover his face in mock embarrassment, but it was too late.

"Am I late?" he asked, climbing the wall of the pier.

"No, I think I was a little early," I said.

"Did you think I wasn't coming?"

"That's a loaded question. I refuse to answer it on the grounds it may incriminate me."

"You're being evasive," he said.

"No, I'm being Irish," I shot back.

"Do you remember coming here the night I met

you?" He settled down beside me.

"Now that you mention it, I do."

"Do you remember how cold it was? I was absolutely freezing and I wanted desperately to leave, but I was afraid that would mean I'd have to leave your side."

"I think we ended up going to my house afterward anyhow," I reminded him.

"And then I got offended because you threw me out."

"Liam, it was three o'clock in the morning. I did not throw you out."

"I usually stay out much later than that," he said. "I have with you many times since then."

"I know," I said. "Funny that you're just now telling me you were offended. You've never said anything about it before."

"I know what you must think of me, Hailey." Liam looked out toward the sea. He took a good long pause and then continued, "I've told you before that I'm new in the ways of love."

"All right, keep talking," I said.

"Well, it's not that easy."

"It's as easy as you want to make it," I said. "Or as hard. Anyway, I'm listening."

"I'm glad you called me to say you're leaving. I was going to call out to you anyway. After I saw you in town, I thought it was meant to be that you and I ran into each other."

"Maybe. I've been turning over this concept of what is and is not meant to be. I don't think it's a casual conversation. I think you and I may have talked about it once before."

"I think we have, yah. I think I was definitely supposed to meet you, though." He seemed sincere.

"Why do you think that?"

"Because I've learned so much."

"Like what?" I couldn't imagine.

"About men and women; about the nature of love. I think love should be unconditional. So many people have it all wrong. People give in order to get, you know. They think, for instance, if I do this, then I'm supposed to be treated this way, and it's always contingent upon something. It's never enough just to love."

"This is what you've learned from me?" I was trying not to sound hurt.

"Yes, most definitely," he said.

"How did you learn that from me?"

"It was more like I learned it at the hands of you," he clarified. "Do you remember when I told you that I was confused?"

"I'll never forget it, and by the way, I realize that I was defensive, but you were scaring me."

"I know. You practically threw me out again," he said with a laugh.

"Liam, allow me to be frank: if someone you've known for a while on a romantic level turns around and tells you they're confused, it's usually not good news. How was I supposed to take it?"

"By not jumping to conclusions. If you'd given me a little more time, I might have been able to tell you something."

"What would you have said?"

"Well, I don't know," he said quickly. "I would have said something like I didn't know where things are going with you and me, and I was unsure about things because I've never done this before, something like that. I was afraid. I didn't know how to protect myself."

A memory came back to me, spontaneous and unbidden, of the night Liam and I had walked in the rain to the sea. He'd looked up in the sky and pointed out the birds coming back to the sea. "They're coming back from inland," he had said. "They always seek shelter from the storm." I realized now, this is exactly what Liam had done; cautious and birdlike, he'd sought refuge from the storm of his own emotions, yet what he told me now seemed like cerebral rationale.

"I don't think you can rationalize love," I said. "I'm not even sure you can put it into words. I don't mean this to sound critical, but honest to God, Liam, you're so much in your head. You can't always figure everything out, I mean, you don't have to figure everything out. Love is about the heart, not the head."

"Well, I've never been in love before." He shrugged his shoulders. "I'd like to be because everybody speaks so highly of it."

I listened to what he was saying and was still confused. I wondered if his intentions were to tell me he had never been in love with me.

"Let me say that again." He paused. "Until I met you."

I got it. I thought maybe I should sit with that one for a while. "Why did you never come back to see me?" I finally asked.

"I figured you didn't want me to, and if I did, I would have to really talk about what I was feeling. I wasn't prepared to do that."

"But why not?" I was exasperated.

"I told you, I've never done this before." Neither of us said anything for a moment.

"I feel like we've wasted time," I said.

"Maybe not. You're leaving now; it would have been harder."

"Meant to be?" I quoted his words.

"Quite possibly so," he said, his voice trailing off.

I kept looking at Liam thinking I probably shouldn't say what I was thinking because it wouldn't change anything if I did. What I was thinking is you make your choices in life, and they dictate everything. It's all about how you handle things in the moment; that's what adds up and shapes our lives.

"What time do you leave on Thursday?" he changed the subject.

"Twelve o'clock."

"How will you get to the airport?"

"Deanna Rader. She's enlisted Bernard O'Malley to come with us," I said. "Where is Shannon airport? About an hour or so away?"

"Closer to an hour and a half." He paused. "I'll be going to America in two months."

"For what?" I was a little surprised.

"I'm going on tour with an Irish band. We have a manager who's touring us across America. We're going to be playing everything from Irish festivals to concert halls."

"Will you be going to California?"

"Yes, we're going to Santa Cruz. How far away is that from Los Angeles?"

"Pretty far. Santa Cruz is on the central coast of California and Los Angeles is in the south," I said.

"Ah, then," he said. I waited.

"Maybe if you were kind enough to leave me with your address, I could contact you before I come?"

"Okay. I'll give you the address of where I'll be working. I'm going to have to figure out where I'll be living once I get there."

"You will think of me," he said. "Or maybe that's presumptuous. What I mean to say is that I think of you often, really. Do you still think of me?"

"Yes, of course I do."

He sat looking at the ground before him as if he were contemplating something deeply.

"Now then, about dinner," he finally said. "I don't think I've ever taken you out to a restaurant."

"You haven't, but I don't hold it against you. You and I have been too busy learning at the hands of each other to be bothered with anything else," I said.

"I'll give you the last word on that," he said, standing up and taking my hand.

Liam and I drove into Galway and went to Le Graal. He ordered a bottle of red wine, and we had dinner by the fireplace in the front room. We did not talk further about the two of us, the nature of love, or missed opportunities. It seemed there was an unspoken agreement to keep things light and pleasant. As we talked, I studied his face until it was indelibly etched in my mind. I did not know what the future would bring, but I wanted to be sure, at the very least, that I'd remember every little detail of his face.

Epilogue

Still

You ask me if I think of you
And I think of you now,
Dreamy in a corner, a cloudless night
Freezing by the sea,
Too uncertain to disturb it
In fear it would all disappear

And I think of you now, jet-black hair defying
reason,
For heaven bestows too much
Of grace of poise of dignity,
For one to possess all three,
To go beyond necessity

But there you are beyond the call
And I think of you there apart from it all
This I would speak if I thought it best you knew
But beauty is often something unnamed
And you are to me beauty through and through.

You ask me if I think of you still,
And all I can be is still,
And think only of you.

About the Author

Claire Fullerton hails from Memphis, Tennessee and now divides her time between Malibu and Carmel, California. She is a three-time, award-winning essayist, a contributor to magazines, and a multiple contributor to a worldwide book series.

She is a former newspaper columnist and radio disk jockey, an avid ballet enthusiast, a lover of German shepherds, and wife to an endlessly patient husband. Currently she is writing her third novel.

To learn more about Claire and her books, please visit her website at www.clairefullerton.com.

Author Acknowledgements

From the bottom of my heart, I thank the following for their generosity of spirit as this book took shape:

Bill Feil, Harriet (Bootsa) Runkle, Louise Wilbourn Collier, Tim Monaghan, Ellen Comesky, Jennie Muller, Lu Anne Fairly, Mark Roebuck (an incomparable musician) and his lucky wife, Julie, Laura Sanderson Healy, Kelly Fisher, Rory Olsen, Ilyssa Adler, Tama Dudley Harris, Louise Pidgeon, Lili Booth, Dawn Carrington, and always my Irish posse.

Dear Reader,

If you enjoyed reading Dancing to an Irish Reel, I would appreciate it if you would help others enjoy this book, too. Here are some of the ways you can help spread the word:

Lend it. This book is lending enabled so please share it with a friend.

Recommend it. Help other readers find this book by recommending it to friends, readers' groups, book clubs, and discussion forums.

Share it. Let other readers know you've read the book by positing a note to your social media account and/or your Goodreads account.

Review it. Please tell others why you liked this book by reviewing it on your favorite ebook site like Amazon or Barnes and Noble and/or Goodreads.

Everything you do to help others learn about my book is greatly appreciated!

Claire Fullerton

Plan Your Next Escape!

What's Your Reading Pleasure?

Whether it's captivating historical romance, intriguing mysteries, young adult romance, illustrated children's books, or uplifting love stories, Vinspire Publishing has the adventure for you!

For a complete listing of books available, visit our website at www.vinspirepublishing.com.

Like us on Facebook at
www.facebook.com/VinspirePublishing

Follow us on Twitter at

www.twitter.com/vinspire2004

and join our newsletter for details of our upcoming releases, giveaways, and more! http://t.co/46UoTbVaWr

We are your travel guide to your next adventure!

Printed in Great Britain
by Amazon

44597942R00142